MOLLY O

MARK FOSS

Cormorant Books

The publisher gratefully acknowledges the support of the
Canada Council for the Arts and the Ontario Arts Council for its
publishing program. We acknowledge the financial support of the
Government of Canada through the Canada Book Fund (CBF) for our
publishing activities, and the Government of Ontario through the Ontario
Media Development Corporation, an agency of the Ontario Ministry
of Culture, and the Ontario Book Publishing Tax Credit Program.

LIBRARY AND ARCHIVES CANADA CATALOGUING IN PUBLICATION

Foss, Mark, author
Molly O / Mark Foss.

Issued in print and electronic formats.
ISBN 978-1-77086-430-6 (pbk.) — ISBN 978-1-77086-431-3 (html)

I. Title.

PS8611.O787M65 2016   C813'.6   C2014-907689-4
                                                      C2014-907690-8

Cover photo and design: angeljohnguerra.com
Interior text design: Tannice Goddard
Printer: Friesens

Printed and bound in Canada.

The interior of this book is printed on 100% post-consumer waste recycled paper.

CORMORANT BOOKS INC.
10 ST. MARY STREET, SUITE 615, TORONTO, ONTARIO, M4Y 1P9
www.cormorantbooks.com

For Michka

I

FOR A LONG TIME I looked for Candy at red lights. Mine was an intense but kindly stare, one that gave silent permission for a woman to wave tentatively or mouth precious words of confirmation. Something like, "Yes, it's me. I've come home." All I got was an extended middle finger.

On the highway, a fleeting glimpse of a white-gloved hand kept my hope alive for hours. When one possibility disappeared over the horizon or off an exit ramp, another one quickly replaced it. Constant movement and high speed made me feel I was getting closer.

If these women had known how long I'd been looking for Candy, they might have twirled their index fingers at their temples, and then stepped hard on the gas when the light changed. I knew my refusal to give up was a sign of hope, not madness. Of course, it bothered me too that I felt compelled to look, especially as I experienced a profound letdown when the woman turned out not to be her. The only relief from my disappointment was to look again, which only led to further disappointment and a renewed craving to look again.

Now I prefer to drive at night so I can't see anyone at all. If I only looked for Candy on the road that strategy might work, but I search for her in grocery store lineups, at the bank machine, in the back row of my early cinema class at Concordia. Maybe I am crazily optimistic, but I take solace that with the launch of my blog, my days of staring at strangers will soon be over.

MY HOPES HAVE always found their greatest expression right here, two miles from our childhood house. Neither town nor village, Stamp is an unincorporated chunk of Ontario, home to a single crossroad, a feed store, and two churches along the tertiary highway we flatter by calling "the main drag." Most of the three hundred-odd residents live hidden from view on back roads, content to be cut off from the world.

Each time I turn onto the third concession, I imagine how Candy will arrive. She has no choice but to travel this dirt road to reach the Wasteland, either on foot along the grassy border or in one of her vehicles. A black Aston Martin Vantage, the one with an Emotion Control Unit for an ignition rather than a key. Driving in the gear of anticipation and regret, she will take the coupe rather than the convertible because she knows the natural elements will mess up her hair, and she wants to look as impeccable as Kim Novak in *Vertigo*.

Time and space, the most complex concepts to represent in cinema, are mastered on this simple road. It teases with the promise of a short, no-nonsense journey, and then unleashes an array of effects to make the drive seem endless. Dust hovers at windshield level, enveloping vehicles in a thick, impenetrable haze that limits visibility to a few feet. The motion of the tires grinds up new dust, pollinating the gravel so that each time I visit there are more and bigger stones. Boulder-sized stones in the roadway are easy to spot at the low speeds required by the constant sandstorms. On either side of the road, oak, poplar, and elm join overhead to form a perfect canopy that blocks out the sun even on the brightest days. Here I am, crawling along at midday in July with my high beams on, negotiating new obstacles amid the darkness and shifting sands, my eyes trained for a puff of luxury exhaust.

I anticipate the bus shelter at the edge of the Wasteland, a homing device that cuts through mirages stirred up by the shimmering heat waves; it's a time capsule from our child-hood and adolescence. Each of us had a space to express our innermost thoughts on the three-sided shelter. Hoss's wall shows an evolution from *Get Smart* catch-phrases to heady quotes from progressive rock, the more meaningful lyrics underscored twice with black magic marker. In deference to King Crimson, he has sketched puppet strings descending from the roof controlled by an unseen hand — a harbinger of his future abdication from responsibility. My space on the opposite wall is split into two parts by the window. I occupy only the top half, leaving my tiny sister extra room to express herself. Even as my early *Laugh-In* one-liners jammed up against later snippets from Dylan, I left the bottom for her. She never claimed her own wall or took advantage of my offer.

Today, I imagine my sister Candy inside the bus shelter, filling up the empty spaces with poetic descriptions of her life as Molly O. Her words spill forth at the speed of sound, eager to make up for decades of silence. They do not defend or explain her choices, simply lay them bare. Oblique, intense, mysterious. She is dressed in the unmistakable cloche hat and low-heeled boots of Clara Bow, the celebrated "It Girl" of 1927. She is testing whether I remember Bow never had a place in her pantheon of silent stars, demanding that I decode the symbolism. Nothing to it. Candy is ready, not to die, but to resume her interrupted life. This girl is no longer "It." She has stopped running. In the space I left for her below the window, she could draw a huge heart with an arrow through it, an expression of gratitude to me for keeping the faith these long years. She has read my blogposts. She knows my motives are true. Indeed, it is my reaching into cyberspace that brings her home.

But the bus shelter is gone; Joseph has had it quartered, splintered, and hauled away. The cosmic musings of Yes returned to the universe, Dylan's answers tossed into the wind for good, Candy's silence remaining unbroken. She will find her way home all the same. The navigation panel in her Vantage coupe has state-of-the-art GPS.

I know she will arrive soon. Imminently. I sensed it early this morning when a guy with a bloodhound tried to drop his plastic bag into my empty garbage container on the side-walk. Someone does this every week, unless I bring in the container the night before. Most dog walkers in Montreal have no second thoughts about me storing their dog's shit in my backyard for a week. But this guy hesitated; a force held his arm down. A gust of wind pushed the container into the street and the dog howled. It refused to budge, and stared at me standing in my window. Exasperated, the man started to walk away. I think I heard him call out: "Molly!" My brother Hoss would say the wind has talked to me.

As a film professor, well-versed in psychoanalytic theory, and as a brother who dearly misses his sister, I can't help but look for meaning in signs. That I should receive such powerful ones amid garbage and shit is an irony worthy of Molly O. It can only mean that Candy has read my posts, and is at long last on her way.

Do I believe in my dreams? I must.

2

HOSS BELIEVES WE CHOOSE OUR parents, willing ourselves into existence in a particular nuclear family that will give us the lessons we need to grow as human beings. Candy's destiny, then, was foretold; we could do nothing to intervene. There's no fighting karma. This is Hoss at his big-brother, New Age best. Except that his saccharine attempts at reassurance only raise more questions. His theory means we all chose Joseph and Mary as parents and that I chose him as a brother. As the last child, Candy chose us all; she must have known what she was in for. So I have to ask myself what we did to make our sister mute, what she was fated to learn from us. What role did we play in her disappearance? If she knows the answers, and only she would, I wish she would sneak them to me.

THE DAY BEFORE Joseph meets Mary, he is practising for his first solo auction from atop a hillock. He imagines an etching of Christ authenticated as a Rembrandt on the block. His strange chant soothes the animals, which gather at his feet. But Joseph stumbles on a clump of earth and loses his concentration. A gust of wind swirls earth around his feet, rising to his face and into his gaping mouth, delivering a new edge to his voice. The cows stuff themselves with grass to quell an inner ache. The geldings rear up on their hind legs, enraged at what has been taken. He knows he has inadvertently accessed the Tone — an expressive power that his father only ever spoke about in hushed whispers, a gift that last made its appearance in a great uncle who ended his days in an asylum. Joseph does not yet understand the nature of the Tone, but pumped up by some unknown force surging through his veins, he is more confident than ever. Tomorrow he will unleash the full power of his voice on humans for the first time, ending his long apprenticeship. None will resist him. He will transform humble Canadian cattle into descendants of the holy beasts that stood vigil outside the manger. Misty-eyed ranchers will rub dirty knuckles to fight off tears, driving bids up to demonstrate the depth of their faith. Is that someone rustling yonder in the August corn? Only the wind.

Mary is not unattractive at thirty-four. Her chestnut hair, when released from its tight bun for nightly strokes of the comb, is full and soft. Her face has been called pretty. When she believes the compliments, her skin becomes ageless, betraying no hint of the cigarettes she feels compelled to hide from her father. Her green eyes are striking. She has already turned down the hand of two local farmers; one she could love a little, the other not at all. She wants more out of life than cleaning up after pigs.

On the morning of Joseph's first auction, a gust of wind blows open the window of Mary's bedroom, infiltrates her pores. Emboldened, Mary reaches deep into her closet, beyond her everyday clothes, selecting a dress better than her Sunday best.

Her elegance is too refined for the muck and straw of the barn, and the farmers and ranchers spit to show their disgust as she passes. Her cheeks burning, she defiantly returns their nasty glances. Above the sweat, stink, and dampness, Joseph takes the stage, and the venomous looks of one hundred men suddenly shift from Mary towards this upstart in a fedora with a walking stick. Mary is relieved; a bit resentful, too, since contemptuous looks are better than none. As Joseph moves the podium to one side, low grumbles turn to catcalls, especially from the back. How are they supposed to hear the bids without a microphone? He adjusts his fedora, and, confidence shaken, reaches towards the lectern. An inexplicable force holds down his arm. Only when he holds to his convictions and returns centre-stage without a microphone does the force let up.

He starts slowly, his voice firm. The first item is a lot of brooding cows. Nothing special. The ranchers stand with arms folded. "Louder," someone shouts. "Lower," shouts someone else. Joseph stops, and the bidders jerk forward slightly, as if on a suddenly braking train. The hall is strangely quiet, uncertain.

Joseph points his staff into the crowd, gripping tightly before launching into the chant he has been secretly perfecting.

The stream of nonsense words between the numbers takes on the quality of a sonnet, the rhythm and rhyme perfectly calibrated. How these men hated Shakespeare in school, but now their hairy ears perk up, the intrinsic beauty of the sounds sweeping them away.

He alters the colour of his voice, the overtones transforming secular poetry into a sermon. Their wives and children still go to church, and these men all profess to be believers, but they have no patience for preachers. This voice shakes them to the core, convincing them that owning these sacred cows can relieve the emptiness of their sorry lives. And so it comes to pass that more than three-quarters of the men start twitching their noses, scratching their temples, rubbing their eyelids — anything to get Joseph's benediction.

His gaze keeps returning to Mary, who stands between her father Willem and Nose-Scratcher, the two high bidders. Each time Joseph catches her eye, his voice takes on a richer hue, his pace quickens. She blinks frequently. He reads this as a sign of love.

They need an obstacle to overcome, a competitor to vanquish. An unexpected cross-breeze tickles the cheek of the Nose-Scratcher's son, giving him an itch to smile at Mary. She turns away, wary because of the crowd's earlier rage. She is weighed down with unknown feelings for this strange auctioneer whose glance holds her in thrall. Enraged at her rejection, Son of Nose-Scratcher stomps mud at her feet, which flows up the full length of her fine coat, even so far as her cheek. Willem flicks the worst mud off his daughter's coat with his bid card.

A cool breeze drifts past Joseph's face, and his voice takes on a darker tone — just as insistent, but with the raw edge of free verse. This time when the ranchers are thrown back to the school room they hear nails on a chalkboard. They clench their jaws and fists, throw defiant looks at this Antichrist on the stage.

Willem has the last high bid, but he is distracted now by the needs of his daughter. Nose-Scratcher senses imminent victory, but Joseph ignores the facial tics that constitute a counter offer. In desperation, Nose-Scratcher tries to lift his arm to draw attention, but a mysterious force holds it in place. None of the four men who step in to help can budge his arm. Joseph looks directly at Mary and declares her father the winner.

The mood turns ugly at this injustice. There is jostling on the floor, grunts and shoves. Haymakers. In the final sequence of *North by Northwest*, Cary Grant lifts Eva Marie Saint off Mount Rushmore straight into the upper bunk of the train berth where they consummate their recent marriage. Joseph Grant holds out his staff over the brawling auction crowd and a part opens, permitting the exodus of father and daughter. They head straight into the church where Joseph takes Mary's hand in wedlock.

You do what you need to do to get born to the right parents.

3

A STYLIZED G, CARVED WITH a router, is featured in the middle of a massive arch that marks the entrance to the Wasteland. A more conventional sign announcing *Grant's Auction Service* hangs just below. This much hasn't changed. Not yet.

I've been living alone now for thirty years and never needed vocal cords to work the microwave. As long as the crab stays at bay, I'll be fine. You deal the cards you're dealt. The Lord giveth. I've had a good life. I imagine Joseph shovels out these que-sera-sera platitudes for my benefit, and that in fact, he roams the Wasteland in the utmost despair, unable to talk even to himself.

Why not blindness from diabetes? Or a heart condition? Deafness, perhaps. Or maybe loss of both legs? No, Joseph has to be stricken with cancer that robs him of his voice, the one function that truly mattered.

His biggest regret, the one that surely gnaws at him through the long hours: the dynasty of Grant auctioneers ends with him. Not with a bang, not with a whimper, but in complete silence. I am using my voice, yes, but what for? Lectures to know-it-alls who text and tweet their way through my experimental cinema course. Hoss is no better, peddling affirmations and other sweet nothings in his polarity therapy practice in Toronto. Instead of squandering our genetic gifts, we could have transcended our humble country origins and risen through the ranks of Sotheby's. Candy's long silence is too big a regret to ponder. Will the long-awaited answers I'm bringing Joseph soothe him or strike him dead?

THE DRIVEWAY SNAKES from the archway back towards our two-storey farmhouse, the house that time forgot. Once inside, I will immerse myself in leftovers from childhood auctions scattered around the living room — the blond Predicta television that no longer swivels, the once-coveted now-sagging beanbag chair, the overwrought iron fire tongs reproduced from the eighteenth century.

Upstairs, the bunk beds that never attached still mark out territory for me and Hoss. Joseph's massive four-poster bed and canopy, which belongs in a Laura Antonelli sex farce, has aged gracefully. In Candy's homage to the silent screen, Marlene Dietrich watches from the wall in top hat and tails, smiling her androgynous smile for the ages.

But it's the lingering traces of older generations that move me most. The banister polished from the grip of countless hands over the centuries, the stone steps at the entrance worn smooth from the stomp of workboots. On the kitchen wall, a series of pencil strokes marks the annual growth of three siblings who lived in our farmhouse one hundred years before: Isaac, Lewis, and Phebe, born in August, February, and June, the same months as Hoss, me, and Candy. Phebe and Candy, in fact, share the same birth date. This is not coincidence; Joseph was determined to time the births of his children with those of their predecessors. He had set up three parallel tracks on the wall to mark the growth of his own children. It pleased him whenever the six of us were in sync. Phebe's timeline stops before she reaches sixteen. I don't know whether Candy's disappearance at the same age is poetic, predestined, or simply respects Joseph's penchant for symmetry.

WHAT I DO know: Mary, afraid to name her children after dead people, outright refuses the idea of a new generation of Isaac, Lewis, and Phebe living in the same house. She is not keen on Joseph's second idea either, but wants to compromise. Joseph likes *My Three Sons*, and I almost go through life as a Chip or an Ernie. *Bonanza*, though, is his favourite television show. Like patriarch Ben Cartwright, his firstborn will be Adam. But when the Adam character left the show while my brother was in the womb, and my mother feared for what this might mean for her pregnancy, Joseph settled on Eric for a name, the second son more commonly known as Hoss. I am named after my father and the youngest brother on the show, and thus, Little Joe. Having run out of Cartwright boys, he had planned to name the third son after the ranch foreman. Once again the character disappeared from the show while the child was in the womb, but he stuck with Candy anyway, even after Mary died delivering a girl.

Supposing Hoss is right that we choose our parents for the lessons they teach us. Hitchcock knocks off what seems to be the main protagonist early in *Psycho* to mess with our expectations. But what were we thinking, choosing a mother who dies in the first act of our lives?

This was the scene: our mother lay prostrate on the operating table, the doctor slapping Candy's bare bottom three times before he got a reaction — a blink of indignation. Was Candy's muteness the price paid for her birth?

Joseph left Candy in the hospital nursery, collecting her after Mary's cremation. She was no trouble at all, the nurses said. Not a peep out of her, in fact. Eerily quiet. All the other newborns wailed for their mothers, who no doubt slept off their ordeals down the hall. Candy, who had every reason to cry, lay in rapt silence, fixated by the twinkle of the industrial ceiling lights.

Joseph was slow to sign the release forms. Perhaps he still hoped Candy was really a boy or belonged to someone else. Once on the street, he set off at a brisk pace, avoiding cracks in the sidewalk to honour Mary's superstitions. On the bumpy third concession, I held onto Candy tightly and she clutched the fingers in my free hand.

Candy and I both blinked, entering the house, adjusting to the dark cloud of mourners waiting to envelop us. Hoss sat on the stairs, refusing to greet our new sister. She didn't notice his hostility. I was two years younger than Hoss and two years older than Candy, and was already torn between wanting love from them both in equal measure. If I could have brought them together I would have, but the same uncles, aunts, and cousins who just stood circumspect over Mary's mortal remains swarmed her daughter. They remarked on the intensity of her green eyes, tugged at her fingers and toes, made faces and goofy sounds. Candy stayed silent, shooting innocent looks that each relative read according to their own fears. In my case, I wanted to believe she needed me. I feared she might disappear like our mother. If I could only love Candy enough, she would stay.

Joseph wanted to harness the power of his voice, leaving guests envious at the unique love that passed between him and Mary. But the lumps in his throat made his vowels crash into consonants and turned his rolling cadences choppy. The gap between words grew longer. Guests shifted uncomfortably from one foot to another until Joseph shook his head and pointed his staff to the table, commanding everyone to eat. They left Candy alone at last, and I was convinced she winked at me.

4

JOSEPH INSPECTED CANDY AS ONE observes the antics of a stranger's child. Her brown hair and Mediterranean complexion were at odds with the fair look of his sons. Our hair is fine and straight, whereas her curls are thick — anyone who caresses them gets his fingers entangled.

Joseph had to set the alarm for feedings as Candy never cried out for food. Offered a bottle, she sucked absently on the artificial nipple, ready to stop when it was taken away. When Candy burped, her mouth hung open quizzically, and no audible air escaped.

The cartoon about the impresario whose miracle frog never sings for anyone but him made a deep impression on me. I put an ear to the closed door and tiptoed into Candy's room. Her eyes were always closed, but I was sure that as soon as I left she would be happily chattering or singing to herself. I wanted to be part of her pleasure, so I walked to the door, closed it without leaving the room, and then scampered back.

I caught her standing in her crib at last. The corner of her mouth curled up slightly, acknowledging she was caught in the act. I held out my hand and she took it, and I promised to keep her secret safe.

Her silence was impenetrable and, to the rest of my family, intolerable. Not just the lack of tears offended — there were no happy baby noises. A parade of white-bread nannies, each blander than the last, sprinkled talc powder on her feet and bottom, humming softly, trying in vain to solicit a smile. Wasn't it enough that she submitted without complaint?

They plied her with baby toys and, later, with all manner of talking dolls to coax words from her mouth. She pulled the cords to see what inane phrases manufacturers had come up with. The dolls all wanted love, to be held or to be taken out; their limited vocabulary only heightened their neediness. She stripped them of their clothes and accessories, and was disappointed that none ever displayed anatomically correct parts. They remained freaks of nature, bloodless simulacra. What could they teach her?

I dangled a necklace of costume jewellery over Candy's face. She rubbed the false pearls against her teeth, testing their provenance. Yes, they belonged to Mary. We passed the jewels back and forth between our mouths. My tongue searched for a hidden crevice, an imperfection that might contain a clue to Mary's whereabouts, but the surface of the pearls was perfectly smooth. No clues, except the faint traces of Chanel No. 5, Mary's perfume of choice. The more I tried, the more distant Mary became, as if the very act of grasping pushed her farther away. So I tried harder, falling asleep with the pearls wrapped around the thumb in my mouth. Candy sucked the pearls with less intensity, a certain detachment that convinced me she knew something I didn't.

HOSS CALLED OUT in his sleep every night for months after our mother's death. Incomprehensible murmurs gave way to whimpers and then disconnected words, thrown out into the void that divides our beds. I squatted on the carpet near his pillow to decipher the high-pitched warnings, the questions left hanging, the dreamy sighs of acquiescence.

At first I envied him this special communication with our mother. Since he showed no sign of remembering, I decided she must be speaking to me. In the morning, I would listen intently to every slurp of his Alpha-Bits cereal, inspecting the leftover letters at the bottom of the bowl for meaning. I pounced on him the moment he got off the school bus, and trailed him around the house until he shouted at me to leave him alone. In his rising pitch, I wanted to hear traces of my mother's nighttime visits.

My fawning over Candy did not sit well with Hoss, whose initial hostility over the new arrival developed into full-fledged resentment. Not only had he gained an unwanted sister, he had lost a brother. As the odd one out, Hoss dreamt up ideas to win back my allegiance and distance me from Candy. He drafted me into his new boys-only spy club, which had iron-fisted rules against spending time with girls. I spied on Candy secretly, keeping my clandestine notes hidden lest Captain Hoss hand out more demerit points or boff me in the head. Whereas I devoted an entire page to Candy's first attempts at walking, Hoss moved the furniture around so that she would topple over. She was too proud to protest or acknowledge emotional and physical hurt.

I wanted to be a good brother to both Hoss and Candy, but my instinctive desire to protect my sister made me damaged goods for him. This was the quality they both shared, Candy and Hoss: all or nothing. He smirked at my pathetic attempts to win Candy's affections, recognizing, long before I did, that she was a world unto herself. Unknowable, unreachable except on her terms. If she had only written a rule book, I would have learned the code by heart, torn up the paper, and swallowed the evidence.

Television was our one shared experience, the only public setting where Candy's silence was considered a virtue. In our living room, in front of the Predicta, an unspoken truce prevailed over us. Neither Candy nor I protested that Hoss chose the shows. While he and I snorted, chortled, and guffawed at *Batman* and *Hogan's Heroes*, I would steal glances at our sister's impenetrable face for a hint of mirth.

Candy drafted me willingly into her make-believe TV games. Without Hoss around, I played both the suitcase that accuses the housewife of leaving stains on her husband's white shirts and the patronizing narrator. In this reenactment of the Whisk commercial, Candy played the silent housewife. I found great comfort in rendering scenarios as precisely as possible, but Candy was a free spirit, even as a five-year-old. Instead of appearing guilty when I screeched out "Ring around the collar," she slammed down the lid of the suitcase, and — my narrator trapped inside — I had to muffle my accusation. Instead of pouring liquid detergent on the stain, she squished a strawberry on the pocket and wiped juicy seeds all over it. Once she brought out a pair of scissors and made a snipping motion. I adjusted the narration as best I could. "We are having temporary difficulties. Please do not adjust your set." This was where it all began — Candy's silent performances and innate understanding of how to take power from men, and my need to restore normalcy at all costs.

The beginning of Candy's play-acting spelled the end of our temporary truce. In our remote home on the Wasteland, where friends were a school-bus ride away and our auction apprenticeship with Joseph had yet to begin, Hoss lashed out. He told Candy she didn't belong. She was not a Grant. With her dark and curly looks, she resembled neither Joseph nor Mary nor either of us, her brothers. Her chromosomes were all wrong. Hoss got the facts of life talk in science class. He understood these things. I could only think back to my Sunday school lesson about the immaculate conception. If the first Mary and Joseph could experience such a miracle, small wonder that our parents could produce a black sheep.

Candy reacted to Hoss's blasphemy, hitting him where it hurts most. She stood in front of the Predicta, forcing us to watch the screen through her. She sometimes stood behind us on the couch. Not saying anything. Hardly breathing. Yet we both felt her presence, as if she was some otherworldly being from *Star Trek*. It drove Hoss mad, and he flung his arms backwards, towards her last known coordinates.

I liked Candy behind me. I pretended she was our mother, distracted from her kitchen chores by one of our television shows. I heard the squeak of the tea towel she was using to dry a glass. Or I simply sensed her, just out of reach and sight. If I glimpsed the enigmatic look on Mary's face, I would feel more distant so I didn't turn my head. It was enough to know she was there. No, not enough.

ON *BONANZA* NIGHTS, with me, Hoss, and Joseph on the couch, Mary stood a few feet behind us. Apart and a part. Mary waited for the Ponderosa map to curl from the flame in the opening credits before striking her own match. I would catch a whiff of sulfur and the intense aroma of her Tareyton cigarette as small puffs passed overhead, Apache smoke signals. I didn't know the code to interpret what she was trying to tell us. The Tareyton magazine advertisements showed women with black eyes, defiant in their choice of cigarette, ready to fight before switching to another brand. Mary was more resigned to what fate bestowed. Cigarettes loosened my mother's tongue. I watched more than listened, fascinated by the white swirls, imagining shapes that others saw in clouds. Mountains and scimitars, deserts and jet streams, fog on low-lying fields in early morning. Did the smoke carry or push her words into the world? They issued forth in short, nicotine-tinged bursts, excess verbiage filtered by the white tip. Yes. No. Supper's ready. She gave it all up with Candy in her womb, relapsing into a more profound silence. When she did speak, her voice was brittle, naked, and unprotected. If only she had kept smoking, she would have lived.

I wanted Candy to take up Tareytons, Export As, Salems, any brand would do. Just to know she would be behind me, a fine blend of mother and sister. Turning my head to check, only to find she wasn't there, made me ache inside. Finding her, without any sign of Mary and her tea towel, would be worse. So I simply believed she was there, willing myself into a dreamlike state of nervous anticipation, hovering on the cusp of elation. It was only after Candy disappeared that I felt compelled to turn my head to look, over and over. Candy, my Eurydice.

HOSS DOESN'T BUY any of this. He reminds me, not for the first time, that he is two years older. If he can't remember our mother in detail, how can I? I tell him his weed-rattled brain might be missing a few receptors, but without confessing my own doubts. Have I made it all up without knowing? No, it doesn't take much to conjure up someone who was always a ghost.

5

THE SPECIALISTS WERE BAFFLED. CANDY could not or would not talk; we rearranged our lives accordingly.

We were all tired of calling for her from the bottom of the stairs and then waiting, never sure if she heard, was ignoring us, or was out. Joseph was afraid that badgering her to speak would only harden her resolve, so I helped him mount a blackboard on the kitchen wall. He was smart enough not to say anything to Candy. He wrote notes to all of us, and eventually Candy took it over. But if Joseph hoped buying Candy's favour would encourage her to speak, he was sorely disappointed.

THERE WAS SOMETHING more provocative than her stubborn silence: Candy's ability to remain detached from the power of our father's voice.

To me, Joseph was a wizard whose mellifluous chant could sweep me up in the cadence of rising numbers mixed with gentle cajoles, mock astonishment, and dry humour. And this was without him invoking the Tone. The natural warmth of his voice was often sufficient to win over the most reticent bidder.

With bids for a bookcase stalled at five dollars, I watched him throw in a box of *Reader's Digest* condensed books with faux leather covers. His voice took on a ring of elegance and grandeur, suggesting literature in a wood-panelled den, a snifter of fine brandy, and a faithful setter at the foot of a dark upholstered chair. And all those dealers of junk, collectibles, and antiques who hadn't read a book since high school, who were buying items only to resell, whose stores and garages were full to bursting, would nod their heads, tap their noses, and pull their earlobes, raising their bids until Joseph tapped his staff at thirty-five dollars. I felt a pang of loss at the thought someone else would go home with these treasures.

I was mesmerized by his staff, which turned beat-up desks, eight-quart baskets of rusty nails, and miniature animal figurines into a hand-painted Louis XV cupboard, a bone-handled chisel from Asia, and an undiscovered Old Master. A straight thrust held in place for a few seconds was his highest accolade for the winning bidder, a sign of respect for a well-fought battle. A small twirl of the tip was dismissive, used on men whose clothes were too showy and who held their bidding cards up proudly for all to see. Some dealers toyed with him by hiding precious items in the odds-and-ends during the preview or bidding solely to make competitors pay more. For them, he reserved a short, contemptuous stab. I half expected them to turn into toads.

At Candy's insistence, we crawled underneath the lowest tier of the stage to escape the humid summer evenings and the eyes of the patrons. Through knots in the barn boards we could see the regulars lined up in the front row, necks tilted up, towards the stage. As Joseph passed overhead, the weight of his feet pressed the boards downward, almost touching our heads, and the microphone cord slipped between the cracks and offered itself as a noose before being drawn taut and disappearing.

His voice came to me as a summons. It was my job to write down the numbers of the winners on a sheet of foolscap so Hoss would know who was buying what and for how much. I knew Joseph scanned the crowd as he chanted, looking for me. I brought my clipboard, so I was keeping up. It was growing dark and I wouldn't be able to write. Hoss would be waiting.

I couldn't afford to mess up. All I wanted was for Joseph to anoint me with his staff as his true successor, ahead of Hoss. There was no precedent within the annals of Grant family history for a younger son to usurp the first-born. I dreamt of it all the same, willing my timeline on the kitchen wall to jump ahead of my brother's so that I would reach the age of thirteen first. Hoss was already ten years old. I was still two years behind; time was running out.

Sitting cross-legged in the dark, I swayed faintly with the imagined trajectory of Joseph's staff and the firm tap that struck the board above my head. He would move to the second and third tier of the stage soon, and the taps of his staff would become fainter.

In our subterranean chamber, my six-year-old sister mimicked the movements of Joseph's staff, silently reproducing the grandiloquence of his chant. I didn't know whether I was hearing sounds from the speakers or from Candy's mouth. Her irreverence invoked in me nervous, guilty laughter.

I heard doubt in Joseph's voice. Had my apparent absence thrown him off tonight? Or did he sense an interloper below, mocking and draining his power? The crowd turned, became unruly, the bids well below par. He pitched *Monopoly*, *Masterpiece*, and *Stock Ticker* as a group of board games, but their frayed cardboard covers, missing tokens, and soiled cards held no interest for the bidders.

I heard the telltale pause. Tapping into the Tone so early in the evening? In our Sunday morning catechism, Joseph taught me and Hoss that if we are blessed with the Tone, we must never use it recklessly. In all cases, it must be invoked consciously; allowing it to emerge accidentally and uncontrolled could create dire consequences.

If he was contemplating the Tone, Joseph must have been in a bad way. My body shook from the guilt that I was letting him down; it shook from the fear of what my sudden disappearance would mean for my future. Then, like all the buyers on the back lawn, I turned into a wheeler-dealer, filled with a compulsive need to possess at all costs. I was ready to buy risky stocks, build hotels in run-down neighbourhoods, overpay for Old Masters. My upraised hand crashed against the wooden plank above my head. And when the bids stopped at forty-five dollars, I was filled with unspeakable remorse, and gnawed at the sliver in my finger because it felt better to punish myself for losing than to sit with the emptiness.

Through it all, Candy maintained an inscrutable facade. She nudged a ladybug along her palm. She brushed off the dirt that layered her bare feet. She gazed at far-off worlds. Hers was not black sheep defiance, but a natural talent to filter out the hypnotic qualities of the Tone. Her quiet aura helped break the spell that lingered from Joseph's performance. Fully awake, my sense of duty rushed back, and I felt the urge to crawl out with my clipboard. But Candy's new pantomime from the *Clue* board game bewitched me. With a toss of her head and a few hand gestures, she became the voluptuous Miss Scarlet in the library with a lead pipe, proclaiming her innocence with a fluttering of her eyes. I believed her. Anyone would. I was frozen in place, unable to help my embattled father above ground. I needed Candy's permission to leave.

6

THE VAST FRONT LAWN, ONCE SO populated with cars on auction nights, seems particularly bereft today. Every May, I help Joseph plant rolls of fresh sod and by every August the grass has turned a ghastly brown. Yet we keep trying, Joseph convinced that this is the year the roots will take. I like his undying faith in possibility. He has not given up on Candy either.

I call out to announce my arrival, knowing I won't get an answer. Sometimes I pretend he's faking it — that, like Candy perhaps, Joseph has simply decided not to speak. He does not have throat cancer; he's just tired of using his magnificent voice to sell other peoples' junk, and the only way to stop is to stop speaking entirely.

The beeps from the microwave draw me to the kitchen. He's nowhere in sight. I pull out the Swanson Hungry Man Dinner — the homestyle gravy, tender green beans and mashed potatoes of his country fried-chicken meal still compartmentalized, still warm. On the table, his glass of milk is cold. The silverware drawer is open, and the back door — leading to the stage — is ajar.

I call out again, this time towards the barn. I wait for his vigorous *de rigeur* wave from the door. Nothing. I begin to worry, quickening my pace for a look upstairs, and then a formal inspection of the barn. I drive back to the front gate, checking behind boulders. I lay into the horn in his truck, expecting him to appear in an upstairs window wondering what all the fuss is about.

The auction stage in our backyard has three round levels, each slightly higher than the last, connected by ramps. For Hoss, the three tiers have always resembled giant versions of the transporter pods on *Star Trek*. For me, they have been potential landing strips for extraterrestrials. For Candy — I know now — they were springboards to a life of performance.

After I circle the stage a second time, I stand on the top tier, thinking another few feet of height will make all the difference in perspective. North, south, west, and finally east, towards those ten dead acres that lie behind the stage. The frayed yellow rope that cordons off the perimeter of the field glows with the force of an electrified fence. I do not see Joseph standing on the flat rock, and the neighbour's horses graze indifferently. I call out again, cupping my hands as they taught me in Cubs. Joseph has wandered out here, drawn by some inexplicable need to reach this flat perch. He's confused, unable to find his way back. The sun, towering overhead, has played tricks with his eyes. In his fragile condition, he has become dizzy and disoriented, walking deeper into the field. Or else he has panicked and started to run, only to be tripped up by a malevolent clump of earth. I walk along the perimeter of the field from one end to another. Too dusty for footprints. He is lying face down now, somewhere out there, unable to call for help.

Or worse. *The flat rock is farther than you think! Stay on the path! Keep away from the bog!* Did Joseph ignore his own dire warnings from our childhoods and take the shortcut across the quicksand pits? Will I find his arm suspended in mud, his hand reaching out desperately to the heavens?

With the field bone-dry, the quicksand pits will be hard and crusty. But Joseph says there's no telling when the firm earth might give way, or how the sands will shift underground. Nowhere is truly safe, and even the path can turn treacherous. None of us has ever seen the mud sink more than a few inches, and that only in the fiercest storm. Hoss says it's all bullshit, the rantings of an overprotective single parent who worried his children would wander off in the field. So why, I wonder, does Hoss only cross the barrier when he's stoned? And why, on those rare occasions when she entered the field, did Candy stick to the path?

I fill up my water bottle, rifle the drawers for the compass, and pick out a walking stick. Joseph's favourite staff is missing, which makes me more anxious. I loop one end of rope around the beam on the stage and the other around my waist. The wind has picked up, as if in anticipation of my trek. I don a balaclava to keep the dust off my face.

The quicksand pits are a safe distance away, but who's to say they haven't migrated? With each step, I expect my stick to plunge into a bog. The earth holds my weight. The cicadas are screeching from the other side of the fence. Amid the sand swirling around my face and the unrelenting sun, I push on, one foot after the other. The insistent whinnies and snorts of the neighbour's horses keep me from losing my bearings entirely. The compass readings seem wrong and I don't know if I should trust science or my senses. Has it been five minutes or a few hours in the field? When does the present become the past or does it sometimes go the other way around? I call out for Joseph again through the nylon over my mouth. The wind does not respond.

And then I stumble upon him, and he brings me to my knees. He lies on his back, near the flat rock, arms and legs stretched out in snow-angel position. Already the swirling earth has begun to bury him. I have to wipe the sand off his face. His eyes are closed, but his raised eyebrows and wide-open mouth look like an expression of rapture.

I whisper his name.

– Your homestyle gravy and tender green beans are getting cold. We can reheat them. Or take new packages from the freezer. Start over.

The horses stamp, snort, swish their tails; they drew Joseph out here in midday with their horsey racket. They miss his pheromone-induced sermons from the mount, the chant so powerful it banishes flies from their eyes. Did he run blindly into the field, convinced the horses' sheer force of desire would restore his voice? Would it come back, defying the doctors, but just for a moment? A note so pure of heart that when its last echo fades in the wind, Joseph simply lies down in the earth, opening himself to his Maker.

Does the restlessness of the horses announce Mary is waiting, standing on the flat rock with her arm outstretched, as if holding up a bid card? For all those years, his wife came whenever she heard that precise tone in his chant; it beckoned her from beyond the beyond. His voice now silent, he has not been able to conjure her. Bereft, she has willed herself into being. Had he run into the field without a safety cord, so anxious to be next to his beloved again? They shared a connection so intense that it has drained Joseph of what little life he has left.

I WALK BACKWARDS with a firm grip on Joseph's arms, dragging his feet along the earth, trying not to trip over the safety cord, which slackens before me as I near the stage. He is surprisingly heavy and I have to stop for water to quench my thirst, checking over my shoulder frequently to ensure I am on track. Several times I find myself walking parallel to the outside edge of the field. Once, I get turned completely around, and head in deeper. The quicksand pits loom closer. It might be better to wait for help — someone official in a white coat who would push a gurney across the field, hauling Joseph out in a more dignified manner. But I'm unwilling for strangers to intrude on his last journey.

His heels catch on a clump of earth, and the sudden resistance trips me to the ground on my back with Joseph on top. The wind dies and the storm settles. I'm not so far from safety. I push on for the last hundred feet, his body seemingly lighter.

The ramp makes it easy to drag him up to the first tier of the stage. Under the canopy, protected from the relentless sun, I tap the rotting wood with his staff, trying to recapture the old magic and let Candy know we're back.

7

WITH EACH CREAK OF THE floorboards on the stage, I peer down, through the cracks, expecting to see Candy. She may surprise me. She always has. My discovery of her secret surpasses anything she has yet come up with. Knowing that somewhere out there Candy is reading my blog is a pleasure matched only by my sadness that I have arrived too late to share my posts with Joseph. I had to finish my own film so I could present my evidence at once.

For all her various guises, multicoloured wigs, and makeup, Molly O's physical resemblance to Candy can't be denied. Beyond their similar heights, the angular shapes of their faces, the intensity of their eyes and the way they project intelligence, they share the same gait — especially the trademark backwards walk Candy perfected on the auction stage. What's more: Molly O lives out countless scenes that can only have been lifted from Candy's life.

Even now, after studying her films frame by frame, and

appreciating the intelligence at work at deconstructing the codes of silent cinema, eroticism, and porn, I get uncomfortable at the idea of my younger sister taking part in sex scenes, however intellectualized. The devices and techniques used to undercut eroticism only inflame desire for the unattainable. I have no creepy sexual longings for my sister, but it's hard not to be in love with Molly O.

How Hoss will react to my discovery of Molly O is hard to say. As much as I'm eager for Candy to walk through that front door, I first want the chance to show my brother my blog and film. After I win him over with my irrefutable analysis, Candy is free to pull a *coup de théâtre*, walk back into our lives, and prove me right.

Only an hour away from the Wasteland, Hoss is blissfully ignorant of what's gone down with our father. He may well drive back to Toronto without ever putting his inner peace to the test with a visit home, as he's done so many times after other retreats.

If I had the strength, I would haul Joseph into the back of the truck and drive him to the morgue myself. I don't want to scramble, pull, and twist. I prefer to let the firm and gentle hands of the ambulance team wheel him down the ramp one last time. Let them arrive and depart with sirens blazing to give Joseph an exit befitting his stature as the best damned auctioneer in the county.

IF CANDY INHERITED her silence from our mother, her sense of the dramatic moment is all Joseph. This might be why she chose our parents in the first place. On stage, Joseph's chant is a fast-moving river careening towards a waterfall. In the homes of prospective customers, his sales pitch is a gentle pond of lily pads, bulrushes, and cattails that seem still, yet actually move under the surface. His meandering style is scripted down to the last pause — the subordinate clauses that spring from nowhere, the calm reflections, the matter-of-fact observations. As are the accompanying facial tics — the worrisome running of fingers through his greying hair, the affirming tilt of the head, the reflective rubbing of his thin moustache. I observe this performance dozens of times, but still get swept up by his folksy charm.

I remember sitting in the country kitchen of a grieving widow, her adult son eyeing us with ire. Freshly baked apple-cinnamon muffins adorned the counter, left no doubt by the wife of Cyril McInnis, Joseph's main competitor. To counteract the home-baked gesture of empathy, Joseph praised the widow's son, noting the passing of his own wife and the unshakeable bond between parent and child. I tossed Joseph a look of affection on cue.

We walked slowly back to the truck, leaving them the contract to mull over. He tousled my hair, pointed his staff at the geraniums sitting in the vintage wheelbarrow. We took the time to smell the flowers. The choked-up son watching our performance called us back to the porch where we signed on the arm of the rocking chair.

Another time, Joseph brought Candy along, believing a traumatized four-year-old daughter would have an even more compelling effect on an old widow. For once, he thought, let her strange silence serve a useful purpose. Candy squeezed the fruit on the kitchen table. She pulled the old woman's hair. She opened the refrigerator door and turned on the tap. We left the contract with them, knowing they would never sign. On the way home, I'm sure Candy winked at me.

THE ENGINE OF the vehicle pulling into the Wasteland sounds powerful, and the two doors that slam are the right number for an Aston Martin — except I was only expecting to hear one door. Has Candy brought a partner on her first trip home? A son? Joseph would have been so pleased. The Tone, which skipped our generation, might well emerge in the next or the one after. I will know when I hear my nephew speak what's possible.

A short stocky woman and a skinny man with a Samurai knot, both in their twenties, emerge from the side of the house in orange jumpsuits. I was right to bring Joseph out of the field. These two, sweating in their uniforms, can't even push the gurney along the dead grass without stumbling.

They cover Joseph with a standard-issue blanket, hoist him up without so much as a one-two-three, and then roll him back to the ambulance. They don't realize, or don't care, that I've trailed them. She's going on about the performances the night before on *America's Got Talent*, how she could have sung so much better. He starts strumming an imaginary guitar, recalling his glory days in a high school air band. No sirens. They plod through the archway onto the third concession without a farewell honk. I regret not hauling Joseph into the back of his truck, daydreaming that my reckless speed would generate enough wind power to kick-start his heart.

Molly O
The seductive cinema of Mickey Nailand

| Home | Films | Suppositions | About Me |

Mary, Mickey, and Molly
Posted by LJ

Mickey Nailand's oeuvre — his experimental remakes of Mary Pickford films — is both celebrated and castigated by those who remember.

Women are uncomfortable with the uneasy relationship between the empowerment and exploitation of young women.

Intellectual men writhe in their seats, unsettled at the idea they could be watching their daughters and sisters in states of undress.

Coarser men drawn by promises of erotica are aggravated by Godardian jump cuts that undermine titillation and accentuate abstraction.

Silent film enthusiasts decry the campy treatment of the genre, even as they secretly enjoy the in-jokes.

Experimental filmmakers, whom Nailand so seriously cultivated, never truly let him into their club.

Who was Nailand, and did his actress Molly O play a larger role than the credits would have us believe?

Consider that early silent films were written by the likes of Anita Loos, Frederica Sagor Maas, and so many other women whose contributions are only now being rediscovered.

In that spirit, this blog will excavate the story behind the Nailand and Molly O collaboration. Close readings of the films, archival research, and my own musings will break years of silence, arguing that Nailand's work deserves a place in the pantheon of underground/experimental cinema, and that Molly O has secrets of her own to be revealed.

Mickey Nailand arrives in the Lower East Side (LES) of New York City in the mid-1980s from a middle-class family in a hick town in the North Country of New York State near the St. Lawrence River. He takes courses at Millennium Film Workshop and joins the Film-makers' Cooperative, but remains a clean-cut outsider in the rough-and-tumble milieu of the LES. Venues like Films Charas prefer more established experimental filmmakers, or at least those with true LES credentials. Apart from sparsely attended screenings at the Coop itself, or at the RAPP Art Center, Nailand's films are most frequently programmed at ABC No Rio and Naked Eye Cinema. Yet he grows disenchanted since his films are never chosen for programs that tour across the US and Canada. Too well-off for radical artists living hand-to-mouth in rat-infested apartments, too apolitical for filmmakers documenting police brutality, too sexually tame for the Cinema of Transgression or Erotic Psyche schools, and too whimsical for everyone else, Nailand becomes obscure, even by the standards of experimental filmmaking.

In the fall of 1989, however, he somehow negotiates a two-week run for his new film, *M'liss*, at the Bleecker Street Cinema. Advance promotion lands a glowing preview in the *Village Voice*. The male critic argues that Nailand's approach teases out the pedophiliac undertones of the original Pickford version, bringing them into the light for critique. He intimates Nailand's unique style could make him the next Jim Jarmusch.

Intellectuals flock to *M'liss* to see what all the fuss is about. On the third last night of the run, two men are ejected from the screening for indecent behaviour, an event that receives lurid coverage. Sleazy men in dark raincoats fill the rows of the theatre for the last showings. Never mind that much more explicit, and uncritical, fare can be seen in porn cinemas. Nailand never recovers from the humiliation.

Leave a comment

8

ON THE "WHAT TO DO first" page on the government website, I'm relieved to see "grief and loss" as a separate link: it must mean they come later. There's nothing to suggest checking your blog for comments from your long-lost sister is a priority. Nothing says it's not either. Nor is there a rule about referring to the deceased in the past tense.

I stop typing long enough for Joseph's screensaver to kick in: a photo of Candy on the auction stage, while she still dressed as television characters. Her eleven-year-old face is already opaque. In the background, atop the third tier, Joseph looks on proudly, taking time out of his chant to observe his daughter. I've never seen this photo before, which gives me hope there are new stories about Candy to discover and new clues to pursue.

Joseph was two and a half days away from winning an autographed photo of David Canary, the actor who played

Candy on *Bonanza*. He never cared for my ruthless eBay tactics. If he was meant to win the auction, he'd win, he would say. A response laced not with my brother's syrupy karmic beliefs, but rather an old-fashioned respect for fair play. Since when has anything been fair at the Wasteland?

Why he wanted the photo is something else again. It's more proof — if ever I needed it — that Joseph has never forgotten his daughter. But this is not the Ponderosa foreman saddling up a horse from our Sunday evenings in front of the Predicta. No, it's a promotional photo of the silver-haired actor from his long career on *All My Children*, the soap opera. Had Joseph's obsession with Candy surpassed my own?

From the bookshelf in the corner of the living room, I bring down musty binders, refuse from a long-ago auction. They are marked alphabetically, although W for will and F for funeral are both empty. Inside the thick C binder, I discover clippings on David Canary, recent research on throat cancer, yellowed news reports on my missing sister, and a contract for cremation with other legal documents clipped to the inside.

How many months did I beg Joseph to plan ahead? Not only has he named Hoss as power of attorney, my brother is also executor of the estate. I am six feet even and Hoss is two inches' taller. Nothing ever changes.

HOSS ALWAYS GOT THE NEW jobs first. Whether it was numbering bid cards with a black magic marker, handing them out to patrons as they arrived, writing down bids on foolscap or taking in money, each task took on a special quality while under Hoss's care and then, once discarded, was dismissed as childish. I could never catch up to a coveted position because Hoss rubbed the shininess right off. The worst of it: I knew he was always wrong.

When he reached the age of ascension at thirteen, Hoss became truly insufferable. He devoted himself to new chores, just like Disciple Caine in the Shaolin temple on *Kung Fu*. Before school and then again upon his return home, he swept the auction stage to keep it pristine. On auction days, he mopped the stage down and climbed on a stepladder to brush off leaves and sticks that fell onto the canopy. He set up the microphone on the top tier of the stage, positioned the speakers, and recommended placement of items. Heavy appliances were on the lowest level. Medium-sized items — Admiral's Lamps, antique scythes and armchairs — were typically positioned on the second level, leaving the highest level for the smallest and lightest items — dishes, books, odds and ends, framed landscapes, conversation pieces. Yet there could be variants, depending on Joseph's mood and intuition, so Hoss needed to back up his suggestions with sound reasoning. Sometimes he miscalculated on purpose, putting the Hollywood pinball machine on the second tier, just high enough that latecomers could not see the faces of Laurel and Hardy under the glass. Sure enough it didn't sell, and Hoss made room for it in the barn. During winter auctions, he draped it lovingly with a blanket so no one thought it was up for grabs.

The voice had to be carefully tended, Joseph told us. I watched as Hoss prepared a honey mixture for Joseph every evening, bringing it to him in front of the television. Candy, who had taken over the beanbag chair, ignored the hand-off. Her gender left her on the sidelines of the apprenticeship process, and she betrayed no interest in arcane father-son rituals. Hoss could not imagine that Candy was to blame for the loose spout on the honey dispenser. He made me clean up the huge dollops of honey that gushed into Joseph's glass. Only Candy and I knew the truth, and it stayed with us, her act of derision unacknowledged.

Hoss was under strict instructions not to attempt the chant himself until his voice broke. Was it youthful impatience, an adolescent urge to rebel, or a desire to prove himself to the Master on his own terms that made him forge ahead, practising the chant in the barn when he thought no one was around. I spied on him through a knothole, admiring his diction as he sped through the nonsense words. Faster and better than I could ever have done, if I ever got the chance. By the time my apprenticeship began, Hoss had secured his place in Joseph's affections. I was relegated to a lifetime of unloading dirty ringer-washers and beat-up goalie pads, waiting for Hoss to be sick so I could take over.

I whipped around in time to detect a blur of motion from Candy's bedroom window. And then another. Rox was over. Again. They had been inseparable since she moved into one of the few houses on our desolate road. At the age of eight, Rox shared Candy's olive skin and dark complexion, but her long black hair was straight and she stood two heads taller. Her voice was not fully mature, yet its depth already shook the teacups if she spoke too loudly in the kitchen. She treaded carefully, cautious about the impact of her words. Once in Candy's bedroom, however, in the midst of their TV commercial reenactments, she unleashed staccato, window-rattling laughter. No doubt Rox enjoyed how Candy gave the male narrator his comeuppance. Without bursting into their room, it was impossible to know whether Candy was amused beyond the usual uptick of her lips or raised eyebrow. Holding up a glass to the wall, I heard the mock serious voice of Rox intoning "Is she or isn't she? Only she knows for sure." She transformed a world where the hairdresser knew best into a declaration of women's empowerment with Shakespearean and Decartian overtones. Candy would refuse to scour the oven or spray it with Mr. Muscle, and Rox played an affronted male narrator. The vibrations from Rox's laughter shook the glass from my ear, so I never heard whether Candy responded in kind. All I knew for sure was that Rox had become Candy's favourite, in the same way that Hoss had privileged status with my father. I didn't know which irked me more.

Hoss was the one who opened the door to Joseph's bedroom to find the two girls in front of the mirror with a bottle of Chanel No. 5 in Candy's hand. I heard the shout, the shriek from Rox, the slamming of doors. Instead of gluing my ear to our common wall, I ran my nose up and down her door, risking slivers in my desperation for a trace of our mother, telling myself it was a game, but not being able to turn away.

For Hoss, Candy's act was sacrilegious, a desecration of the holy shrine left on Mary's dresser. I was more circumspect at this sign of interest in our mother. Perhaps Candy would come to me next, and I could share what I remembered. It would have brought us closer.

MY MEMORIES REPLAY with no script changes allowed. I am mired in the same feelings of ridiculousness for wanting to be my sister's best friend. The only addition permitted is a sense of dread, a helpless desire to know where we all veer off course and to get everyone back on track.

Molly O
The seductive cinema of Mickey Nailand

| Home | Films | Suppositions | About Me |

The underbelly of eroticism
Posted by LJ

Following the fiasco at the Bleecker Street Cinema, Nailand abandons LES for West Saugerties, famous for its link to Bob Dylan's *Basement Tapes*. He makes four more films with Molly O before dying of heart failure at the age of 38. He is buried in his hometown of Shepardsville, New York.

Molly O, too, disappears, leaving many unanswered questions.

The scripts bear such a feminist sensibility it's difficult to imagine Molly O has no input. Yet she is given no credit. Does she prefer anonymity or is the sexual tension in their art informed by creative tension in their lives? The nature of the films demands trust and intimacy, but does this extend off the set?

Asked about her relationship with Nailand, his death, and her decision to leave the film industry, Molly O apparently hands the reporter a note that reads: "I have the right to remain silent."

The arrival of "talkies" ends the careers of so many giants of the silent screen, but they only have a few years left before a younger generation takes over. Women who take their clothes off, even in experimental films that blur body parts beyond recognition, can expect an even shorter shelf life. At Nailand's death, Molly O is in her twenties. She could seize her flash of fame to work with other experimental filmmakers or take a stab at mainstream Hollywood. Instead, the lady vanishes. She is far too young to have ended up a recluse like Greta Garbo. Is she preparing a comeback, like Norma Desmond in *Sunset Boulevard*? Is her silence compulsive habit, conscious choice, or genetic inheritance? Perhaps the time has come for her to step backwards into the past, and break her extended silence.

Leave a comment

9

I STOCK UP ON JOS. Louis cakes for Hoss, in the event he keeps his promise to visit the Wasteland after the retreat. He has sworn off junk food and weed, but the news of Joseph's passing may send him over the deep end.

In the dead space between aisles, a cart poking its cage tentatively around the corner stops me in my tracks. Seconds later, the back of a short, curly headed teenage girl makes me do a double take. Never mind Candy never liked this store, and that she's in her forties by now. This is how my mind works, and I can't turn it off.

SERIOUS BIDDERS MAPPED out what they wanted during the preview, but Joseph felt the theatrics added drama. So Hoss walked up and down the stage, holding items or standing beside them as Mary once did. Hoss looked good up there and he knew it. All business — discreet, respectful, efficient — the perfect complement to Joseph's chant until a growth spurt rendered him gangly and uncoordinated.

One night he picked up a wrench, and dropped it immediately, narrowly missing his foot. Once retrieved, he kept tossing the tool between his hands as if too hot to handle. He did the same with the rasps, the plane, and the crowbar. He came across as a clumsy goof who couldn't hit a nail straight or read the bubbles in a level, exactly the opposite image that Joseph was trying to evoke with the gruff, masculine, handyman edge of his chant. Hoss peered down at me in the pit with my foolscap, and I read fear on his face.

Joseph, too, sensed something was wrong. He switched in mid-chant to pitch hand tools with rubber or plastic handles; Hoss had a better time of it. Even so, when a bidding war erupted over a Royal Doulton figurine, Hoss was hard-pressed to hold the piece for more than a few minutes. For the rest of the evening, Hoss pointed to small items rather than picking them up, which made him look ridiculous.

His hands emanated heat for no apparent reason. Touching metal was the worst, but even wood product burned him. In the kitchen, while Hoss ran his hands under cold water, Joseph told him that premature chanting has been known to produce exactly this effect on the metabolism. His Great Uncle Harold was left with stigmata on his wrists after lifting a bandsaw; he had to wear gloves and long-sleeved shirts thereafter.

Hoss professed innocence. Candy and I pretended we were none the wiser. Did she hold her tongue because she knew what would happen, and how it would propel her to stardom?

Did she secretly hold a soft spot for Hoss and want to protect him? Or was she above the petty concerns of her brothers and the rest of the Grants?

Hoss started smoking weed to relieve the stress. A mild buzz cooled his outer extremities long enough to hold the same object for up to ten minutes; it calmed his limbs so he could walk without tripping. I wasn't sure if it was the weed, the premature chanting, or a mixture of both, but Hoss's fourteen-year-old voice was trapped in an upper octave a notch beyond Jon Anderson, the singer for Yes and, for all I know, the voice of Great Uncle Harold. Joseph said nothing, but neither did he begin Hoss's voice training.

Even as the weed helped relieve Hoss's physical symptoms, it instilled a profound sense of detachment. The narcotic effect enhanced the dreamlike elements of Joseph's delivery, putting Hoss into a trance. He held up a set of used wrenches, a rake, or javelin darts long after the bids closed and I'd noted the winner's card number. When bids opened for a washer and dryer, and Hoss pointed to a lawnmower, he became a liability. He knew it, too. I thought that was why he smoked more than usual the night he fell off the stage. It provided an honourable exit.

The failure of an apprentice was unprecedented in Grant auctioneer history, and created a dilemma for Joseph. I was still a year away from ascension, and Joseph could not bear to promote me prematurely — not after what happened to Hoss. Candy was too young to take in money. He didn't trust Hoss around the cash or anything else. As Joseph pondered his next move, I swept the stage before and after school, thinking this mix of humility and ambition would turn the tide in my favour.

Except that Candy and Rox emerged from their long, private apprenticeship of play-acting for the bright lights of the auction stage. With Rox egging her on, Candy dressed like a TV hostess and displayed an afghan covered in cat hair as if it were a coveted prize on *The Price Is Right*.

It's only for a year, Joseph reassured me. Until Candy turned eleven and I turned thirteen.

10

I WAS PROMOTED TO HANDLE sales behind the card table. Rox took over my job, writing down winning bid numbers, a tacit acknowledgement that she was nearly family. More than Hoss, who was excommunicated for falling to the ground from the second tier of the stage, stoned. He responded by upping his weed intake, feigning disinterest in his change of fortunes and heightening his commitment to interpreting the lyrics of Yes and Genesis. I was caught between my siblings. I wanted everyone to get what they wanted, with no trade-offs. Or so I told myself. Behind my earnest and helpful gaze, I scanned Rox's list of winning bids eager to find a mistake. All her columns were perfect. She drew little images beside the numbers. Who could compete with such artistry?

There were no extravagant, Cher-like costumes for Candy's debut, just a simple pair of slacks and a flowered top, taken in to fit her tiny frame. I recognized them.

Everyone did. In the midst of a chant to sell a CB-radio, the Tone emerged, unbidden and uncontrollable. Joseph's steady stream of words snagged on hidden shoals, breaking into syllables, deconstructing into constituent parts. His voice tapped into every crevice of craving in those men's hearts. Some upped their bids, desperate to conquer and possess. Others felt a sudden rush of desire, and then a flush of shame as they saw the ten-year-old on the stage.

As Candy twirled the knobs, I heard Mary's name wrapped in longing, pouring forth on all channels. I did not want it to stop, and when the bids closed out at three hundred and twenty-five dollars, I was shaking with grief and loss at the emptiness that followed. Staring up at this spectre of Mary on the stage, I waved madly to get her attention. Here I am! Over here! Sweat splashed into my face with each movement of my arm, making my eyes sting and water.

Joseph, too, was spent, rushing through the rest of the items lest he break down in public. It was the best take in years, which he attributed directly to Candy's stage presence. Even so, he packed up Mary's clothes from the bedroom to prevent any further reincarnations — as if this could excise her from our lives.

CANDY'S ESSENCE REMAINED hidden from all of us through her silence, and her stage presence became an extension of this mystery. Hiding in plain sight, she disappeared into an endless parade of characters, each amplified by Joseph's delivery. For her game-show-host look, his chant sounded like the off-screen pitchman who describes what a lucky contestant has just won. Amid the flow of nonsense words between the rising bids, I was sure I could make out "A trip to Hawaii!" and "A brand new car!" The chant wrested men out of their comfort zone, teased another one-last-bid out of them so they could see what was behind Door Number Two.

When Candy took on the androgynous look of Twiggy on the catwalk, Joseph's rhythm and Cockney accent captured the swinging sixties, and the men overpaid for mouldy fur coats, mismatched suits, and stained Bermuda shorts. Joseph's languid tone managed to evoke a psychedelic experience when Candy emerged in bell-bottoms, tie-dyed T-shirt, and a daisy in her hair. The farmers forgave the worst excesses of the sixties and casually raised their bid cards towards marmalade skies. Candy was careful to sprinkle more down-home characters into her repertoire. The junk dealers were particularly enamoured of her rendition of the dumb blond country girl from *Hee Haw*, even if the cleavage was fake, while the more genteel appreciated the big-haired, Champagne Lady from *The Lawrence Welk Show*. All Candy's characters wore gloves, an effect that ranged from sublime to absurd.

I kept my distance, pretending I had a choice.

Her wardrobe for the evening performance was a closely guarded secret between Candy and Rox. In this old farmhouse on the third concession, these pre-teen girls developed a mocking, postmodern sensibility — delivering an evolving commentary on the social construction of women totally out of keeping with their surroundings, age, and experience. Was it intuitive, inspired by the contempt of the men in those ring-around-the-collar commercials? Maybe an extraterrestrial landed on the pods in the backyard and beamed this knowledge through Candy's bedroom window.

ON THE MORNING after yet another school-night sleepover, the girls walked back to Rox's house down the road. Even in fine weather, they waited out of sight in the bus shelter, deflecting my attempts to spy on them. Hoss was in tenth grade and was picked up by older high school friends who drove. I was tall enough to scribble profound sayings on the ceiling of our shelter, but would gladly have fought over creative rights rather than face the solitude of the daily wait for the bus. Thinking about what Candy would do next filled the empty space.

I wondered if our counterparts — Isaac, Lewis, and Phebe — learned their letters in a one-room school house, walking the miles hand-in-hand, humming the tunes of the day in three-part harmony.

The bus picked me up after the girls, who sat directly in the middle rows, the better to invoke the hate of all the other eleven-year-old girls in front and behind them. Those country hicks took Candy's silence for superiority rather than indifference, and resented that she communicated in a coded pantomime which only Rox could understand. The boys teased Rox for her early breasts, which she tried unsuccessfully to hide in oversized sweaters and behind her school books. The girls focussed on her voice, which had developed into a powerful instrument. If not entirely silent, Rox spoke sparingly. Her words built up inside before they gushed out, a deeply masculine rumble that swept homework off laps and into the aisle three rows away. They taunted her, trying anything to make her speak so they could laugh at the tsunami effect. I felt every kick and punch against the backs of their seats. They didn't know I was silently fighting for them, and surely wouldn't have cared if they did.

AT THE AGE of ascension, I began chanting practice after my voice broke. Joseph, who was just as entranced by Candy as everyone else, took little notice of my development. He had a secret weapon in his daughter, and no need of a son to succeed him. Candy would continue to dazzle patrons for years to come. This was what he thought. We all did.

The first two years of high school were unbearable without the presence of Candy and Rox. Hoss, the prog-rock stoner entered his senior years, acknowledged my presence at school only to hit me up for loose change to cap the munchies. I stopped reproducing Dylan quotes on the ceiling of the bus shelter, and instead stroked off days until the girls' arrival with a black magic marker.

When the girls started high school, and we all took the same bus again, nothing and everything had changed. The tormentors were two years older, but their underdeveloped imaginations were still mired in schoolyard taunts. "Slut" and "Lezzie" were the best they could do. Candy and Rox responded, if at all, through amplification, cuddling up to each other on their seats.

At the orientation for new students — a mock slave auction — the other grade-nine girls wore low-cut tops and batted eyes at the senior boys, desperate to carry their books around for the day. Candy and Rox stunned the room into silence by arriving in blackface and torn dungarees. The vice principal, whose amateur chant was already a half stutter, lost his good-natured chuckle. Sensing an attack on the school's hallowed traditions of afternoon exploitation, he coldly proceeded to sell the girls off.

Most potential slave owners seemed worried about the girls' unruly character. There were only two of us, me and an unknown opponent in the back row. I suspected it was Hoss, eager to punish Candy for her perceived slights against his character all these long years. Not me. I would be a righteous man with a good heart, fair in my demands, respectful of their proud lineage, accepting of their peccadilloes.

Knowing his need for weed would prevail over all other concerns, it was easy to outbid Hoss. I won the girls for seventeen dollars. Except after one look into Candy's green eyes, I released them unconditionally. Emancipated, they showed no gratitude for my selfless act. Why should they have? They were free spirits.

II

HOSS AND CANDY DEVELOPED A remarkable talent for mutual avoidance, as if they had sat down and mapped each tour around the halls with military precision. I admired their tenacity, single-mindedness, and resolve to have nothing to do with each other. Then there was me, volunteering for self-appointed reconnaissance and spy missions. How often Candy and Rox passed through the corridor of the cafeteria during lunch hour. At what times they stepped out for breaks in the smoking area. When Candy wore jewellery pilfered from our mother's dresser rather than auction leftovers. It all got stored, this useless intelligence, for the day that more advanced technology could interpret patterns for meaning.

I followed them on their tours through the school, observing the turned heads, the open mouths, the hateful gazes. They passed a group of girls standing by their open lockers. They sniggered, and, putting on their best Cher voices, sang the opening line to "Gypsies, Tramps, and Thieves." Candy was the tramp. Her green eyes had grown deeper, her olive skin darker, her curls more seductive, her mouth more immovable, and lips fuller, as if borrowed from the face of a Hollywood starlet. Her slinky houndstooth dress, vintage Bakelite earrings, and saddle shoes were completely at odds with her peers' factory outlet jeans and T-shirts. Rox, with her calico dress, bohemian shawl, and Gitanes, was the gypsy. I was the thief, flitting unnoticed through the free-for-all of the halls, stealing glances at Candy and Rox. I figured out their schedules, arranged to fall in a few paces behind as they walked to class, never close enough to get caught. It was exhilarating, this game. Better than sitting on the sidelines.

If Candy and Rox were the most outlandishly dressed students in the school, I was the most chameleon-like. My jeans, T-shirts, and checkered lumberjack shirt were perfectly calibrated to disguise me as another tree in the forest. Even so, I didn't have to steal glances, not really. Candy and Rox were so wrapped up in themselves that I could pass unnoticed between them. Some days I thought Candy and Rox had stolen my life. In truth, I had given it up willingly, and they remained blissfully unaware of the gesture. Nor would they have appreciated it. This was what hurt the most.

I was the Grant with the wrong genes. Instead of living up to my namesake on *Bonanza* — the hell-bent, impetuous young firebrand — I was pathetically eager to compensate for the idiosyncrasies of my siblings in the eyes of the teachers. Unless he was stoned, Hoss could not hold a pen or peck at a typewriter without risk of third-degree burns. When he showed up in class, he preferred to talk, waving his hands to

cool them down. He excelled at seminars and class partici-
pation, where he provided both the questions and the
answers. The teachers couldn't shut him up. Candy, they
couldn't get to talk at all. With her otherworldly sense of
fashion, she held her tongue firmly in her cheek, relying on
the written, typed, and chalked-up word. For unavoidable
oral presentations, she worked in tandem with Rox, who
altered her voice slightly to indicate when she was speaking
for her friend. Stuck between my siblings, in eleventh grade,
I strove for the middle ground between too much and too
little of anything.

My bland countenance gave the teachers some relief from
the extreme states of Hoss and Candy. Behind my controlled
exterior, my temperature ran hot and cold, and my vocal
chords were knotted with half-finished auction chants,
stillborn shouts, and unwanted silence. I was a watched
kettle. No one witnessed when my anger boiled over or the
self-recrimination that followed.

There is a scene in every horror film where the protago-
nists are about to do something stupid. We, in the audience,
know it's a mistake. We shout to warn them. We curse. We
wring our hands helplessly. Nothing makes any difference.
The characters cannot outrun their fate.

Beecroft, the science teacher who ran the photography
club, started up a weekly showcase of silent cinema classics.
I told Candy, lamented she was too young to appreciate the
films, and then waited for her to show up to spite me. Of
course Rox joined, and so all three of us saw Mary Pickford
in *The Foundling* playing a character named Molly O.

Molly O
The seductive cinema of Mickey Nailand

| Home | Films | Suppositions | About Me |

Going, going, gone
The Auction Films, Part I
Posted by LJ

Payment for goods and services is never simple in Nailand's films. The cost of everything is always in question, requiring intense negotiations — whether for sex or a loaf of bread — and time is always on the seller's side. The incessant bartering creates a permanent state of unease in viewers, at least those who have seen more than one or two of his films. We know the moment will arrive in a male character's storyline where a speedy purchase will be necessary to achieve his aims, and that a woman will thwart his desires.

Arguably, the back-and-forth over money finds its purest expression in Nailand's two "auction films" where the bang of the gavel announcing a final sale resonates with the moral weight of a courtroom judge. What is Nailand trying to say? That love has no price? Or that sex is always a transaction? One thing is clear: Molly O appears exceptionally comfortable in her roles in the auction films, as if she were born to play them.

In the original version of *Daddy Long Legs* (1919), an orphan girl named Jerusha placed in a boarding school by an anonymous donor grows up to fall in love with the older man who is paying her tuition. In Nailand's hands, Jerusha — played by Molly O — quickly discovers the identity of her wealthy benefactor and his nefarious scheme to seduce her, and hatches a plan to milk him for all he's worth. Exploiting his infatuation with her at Fifth Avenue boutiques, she pushes him to buy expensive items "before the store closes." She even manages to get him to sign over his deluxe penthouse "to save on taxes." All the while, he enjoys free access to her body, without recognizing the true cost of the sex.

In the penultimate scene at an art auction, the man is visibly distressed at the escalating price for a Van Gogh, but seemingly in a trance brought on by the auctioneer's chant. Seizing the bid card from his hand, Jerusha wins the auction. While she hangs *Sunflowers* in her new penthouse home, the man barters for an apple at a food stall — a sly evocation of Marlene Dietrich's "What Am I Bid for My Apple?" sequence in *Morocco*. With the seller — a woman, of course — closing up for the night, he again pays too much. But Jerusha, having outwitted the naive lover and "won," is already bored. Jerusha sits naked at the table, her back to us, pulling off the petals of a daisy in a silent "He loves me/he loves me not" ritual. With the answer still in doubt, the film curiously cuts to the auctioneer walking along Fifth Avenue. He stops, looks up at the penthouse, as if aware of Jerusha's presence, as if it's his love she wonders about.

Leave a comment

12

MARY PICKFORD, THE INNOCENT WITH the curls who demanded top pay and created United Artists with Charlie Chaplin and Douglas Fairbanks. Theda Barra, the original vamp who believed bad girls were never forgotten. Louise Brooks, the manipulative woman-child whose bobbed hairstyle remains iconic. Candy took great pains to imitate her new silent film heroines on the auction stage, leaving behind television characters, commercials, and, essentially, any need for a male narrator to piece it all together.

But still I tried. Despite Joseph's best evocations of Cecil B. DeMille, a Bolex camera, eight hundred feet of 16 millimetre film, and a Steenbeck editing machine went un-purchased. I saved them from the junk heap, offering to film Candy's performances. No, she wanted Rox as her director of photography. No male presence sizing her up, deciding on the frame, determining what parts of her to display. The messy bits, no problem, I could do that. In the school's dark room, under the soft red glow of the safe light, I wound film diligently back and forth through the tank. Not one inch of Candy's performance would be underdeveloped or scratched. Never mind that Rox's first attempts turned out to be shaky hand-helds and laboured tracking shots.

I started up the Steenbeck at the lowest speed, thinking a slower pace would help me learn how to edit more easily, but the film stuttered through the pulleys and rollers until I blew a fuse. Joseph helped me clean the circuit board and the motor, and we shifted the speeds up and down to get the thing running properly, much like we switched the channel tuner of the Predicta back and forth when we lost the signal from a station. The Steenbeck remained temperamental, which made me feel indispensable. I was the only one who could coax it to life. Once Candy realized how much the editor shapes a film's outcome, she insisted I pass on my skills to Rox. Why was I so unfailingly easy to get along with? Where was the indignation, the storming off, the bartering? Was I not the son of an auctioneer? No, I was a stray hair on a lens, clinging for purpose until blown off.

Going, going, gone opened with Candy in a short black dress, a feather boa over her shoulders, carrying a wicker basket, evoking Dietrich's cabaret performance of "What Am I Bid for My Apple?" Holding a Golden Delicious in her palm, Candy played Eve, tempting male auction-goers to discover a new paradise. Much later, Candy appeared in tails to evoke the famous kiss between Dietrich and a woman at the cabaret. This was fuel for the gossip at school about her and Rox. But she went beyond provoking a titter caused by a same-sex kiss to capture, perhaps unwittingly, her true essence. For Candy did not kiss Rox. Instead, she approached a mirror with a knowing look, removed her top hat and stared into her own eyes as she kissed her mirror image. The scene lasted much longer than the viewer's comfort level.

For years, the crowd scenes bothered me. They appeared almost as still photos with no real connection to what was happening on the stage. I studied them anyway, convinced I could find a clue to Candy's disappearance amid the nondescript faces. With a magnifying glass, I examined facial expressions for any sign of menace. Unlike Shakespeare's Globe Theatre and its pit filled with grubby peasants, the three sides of Joseph's stage were surrounded by men of every class. I had pet names for everyone — Gardener, Dealer, Combover, Junkman, Cottager, Bourgeois Cousin, Loser. It was Porky who made me shiver.

The lighting was poor, and his face covered in shadow, but I sensed Porky was an average-looking man, neither handsome nor homely. Too young to be interested in auctions. He crossed his arms against his chest, apparently indifferent. Unlike all the other men who look to the stage and Candy, Porky appeared in all four crowd scenes, standing in much the same way under his pork pie hat — eyes to the camera, blank expression. I didn't like him and what I took as an imitation of Lester Young's elegance. Since he was so focussed on Rox and her camera, my suspicions went no further.

Molly O
The seductive cinema of Mickey Nailand

| Home | Films | Suppositions | About Me |

The Days and Nights of Molly O
Posted by LJ

Molly O's Wikipedia biography reports her real name
as Sharon O'Riley, "from the small town of Deep River,
Ontario." But Deep River is the home of the wide-eyed
blonde played by Naomi Watts in David Lynch's *Mulholland
Drive* — the girl who wins the jitterbug contest and arrives in
Hollywood only to become a disillusioned, broken-hearted
drug addict stuck in bit parts. Someone is having us on.
Molly O's true identity may never be known, although —
like the Lynch heroine — she may well have arrived freshly
scrubbed from small-town Canada, perhaps from one of
the villages and towns close to Shephardsville, the town in
northern New York State where Nailand got his start.

Leave a comment

13

THE GUYS IN OUR HIGH school were weekend squatters in Shephardsville. We were under the influence of boredom and bad taste, longing to escape our country roads and our so very provincial drinking-age laws. The guards at the border waved us through and the bouncers at the bars waved us in. We could not pass for locals — our look was too clean-cut, our gaze too eager, our accent too apparent even against the pounding music. But they accepted our funny money on par with their own greenbacks, and we felt like equals. Superiors, even. Yes, we made friends with trailer-park girls and when one of their fathers went off drinking we stocked up at Jack's Liquors and hightailed it back to their boxes for even cheaper drunks. We were just passing through, and none of us would have wished for the dreary lives we saw playing out. At the end of a Shepardsville Saturday Night, if no one had slashed our Canadian tires, we could easily leave all the tawdriness behind. When I was designated to drive, I held my breath at the border, fearing the supposedly scentless Vodka would give me away or that like in the celebrated opening sequence of *Touch of Evil*, the car would explode as soon as we cleared customs. The edge of danger made me feel alive, and I body-slammed our common wall in the hope of convincing Candy that I existed.

I STUMBLED ONTO Shepardsville again in the most unlikely of places: the study room of the Film-Makers' Cooperative in New York.

Spending my sabbatical looking for Candy at greasy diners across the continent seemed far more interesting than searching for something new to say about *Film*, Samuel Beckett's collaboration with Buster Keaton. I leafed absently through filing cabinets, searching for an unfamiliar experimental film-maker to ignite my old passion. Mickey Nailand, with his Buster Keaton-style pork pie hat, his Shepardsville origin, and his affinity for Mary Pickford, intrigued me. More than that, he looked vaguely familiar. I figured our paths crossed in a Shep bar.

Then it hit me: he is the creepy figure of Porky in the crowd in *Going, going, gone*. Playing the girls' film back in my mind, I finally saw what's not there: Mickey Nailand is not holding a bid card. He did not come to the Wasteland to barter for someone else's unwanted property. No high bid checked off the foolscap. No American funds accepted at par. He came for Candy, and he would take her from us without payment.

I watched *One Hundred Percent American* turned slightly in the swivel chair, unable to experience it head-on. Despite all the oblique clues, I was unwilling to accept the obvious. Because, for all the film's cleverness, it shows a young woman engaged in sexual acts; this is not the future I envisioned for Candy. Later, this hesitation was what ultimately convinced me. An intellectual critique of erotica and porn conventions would have been cheap and smug. Instead, Nailand teases us. He opens the peephole and shuts it again. He refuses to let us forget our baser instincts, forcing us to analyze the contradictions between desire and detachment. The actress embodies this vision with a rare force of eroticism, humour, and intelligence, recreating, expanding, challenging, enticing. Her sensibility, on top of the physical resemblance and the imbedded clues in the story and visual treatment, convinced me that Molly O and Candy are one and the same.

Molly O
The seductive cinema of Mickey Nailand

| Home | Films | Suppositions | About Me |

Ring them bells
The Auction Films, Part II
Posted by LJ

While *M'liss* is Mickey Nailand's most notorious film, *One Hundred Percent American* is his most accomplished. The Pickford original is jingoistic kitsch, wrapping the flag up in a girl, a ball, and Liberty Bonds. Nailand's version of *One Hundred Percent American* depicts a politically incorrect draft dodger — played by the director — crossing the Canadian border for sanctuary.

The draft dodger wants to satisfy the sexual needs of an auctioneer's daughter, but the girl understands quickly that his attentions are more about his own need to control. They go back and forth, like an auctioneer up against a determined bidder, with the familiar refrain of "going once, going twice, sold!" offset against the idea of "coming" once, twice, and three times.

The sex is both explicit and oblique — intended not so much

to tease the audience as to comment on its desire. Black and white, and silent, it uses inter-titles to express dialogue. As if seeing "Oh, Oh, Oh, Yes!" on the screen isn't absurd enough, Nailand inserts the words at the height of the sexual encounter as a kind of seventh veil — to conceal rather than reveal. They appear in ornate calligraphy, recalling the font used in Pickford's films, which heightens the strangeness. The inter-titles are uncredited, but the feminine feel clearly suggests a woman's touch.

To amplify the generic nature of the sex, each encounter the draft dodger has with throwaway lovers is filmed with discarded clothes in the foreground, lingering on designer labels while bodies thrash it out in the background. The sex scenes with Molly O, by contrast, are imaginatively presented; the body parts are equally obscured, but the observant viewer can pick out some object — a lamp, a rug, a hammer — that the auctioneer's daughter had been holding up for inspection. An auction is no idle choice since it's all about buying and selling commodities with the escalating bids mimicking the sexual act.

In the penultimate coupling, the draft dodger is licking Liberty Bell stamps and sticking them all over Molly O's body — on banal parts, as well as erogenous zones, making the viewer question why nipples are any more erotic than knuckles. Yes, the Liberty Bell is "cracked," but Nailand has enough taste not to make any visual puns to remind us.

"I will bring you to the Land of the Free!" mouths the draft dodger. Molly O's body vibrates from his attentions, either

out of sexual arousal or in response to the sound waves
of all those Liberty Bells ringing on her skin.

"More!" she silently mouths, and we're left to wonder if she
wants to be stamped for sexual titillation or to secure passage
back to the United States. With the final stamps, he strings
five bells across Molly O's lips, and her muffled protest —
playfully rendered onomatopoetically in the inter-titles as
Whmmhhh thmmmm fummmm? — reveals his true intentions.
The draft dodger, fleeing the imperialist politics of his own
country, blithely imposes his own brand of democracy
on "the other." Molly O, refusing to be silenced by this
patriarchal nationalism, rips the stamps off her mouth.

"No good here," she mouths. Is she condemning the intrusive
foreigner in her midst? Criticizing her home and native land?
Or wryly informing her arrogant lover that US stamps are not
accepted in Canada?

With her father and the Mounties closing in on them, the two
flee the country, crossing the border by boat in the dead of
night. In a hyper-real climax that only underscores their futile
predicament, Nailand leaves them in an abandoned house in
northern New York State with a full refrigerator, a warm fire
crackling, and American hundred-dollar bills stuffed into the
cracks of the windows to stop the draft. It's a perfect ending,
although the sentimental among us might long for an echo of
Daddy Long Legs, a return to the auctioneer alone on the stage,
bereft at the loss of his daughter and extraordinary assistant.

Leave a comment

14

THE THREE OF US TRAVELLED in singular orbits, rarely crossing each other's path. Candy continued her triumphant appearances twice a week on our backyard stage with Rox aiding and abetting, while I handled administrative tasks. With her increased confidence, Candy became more reclusive than ever, taking trays of food to the bedroom for Rox and herself. I imagined they planned the next day's wardrobe, either for school or the stage. Their secret world on the other side of the bedroom wall no longer enticed me. By grade thirteen, I stopped following Candy's trail in the school corridors and fuming silently at her exalted status on the auction stage. Let her model those ratty faux-fox stoles: I took my life back, and was grateful, not resentful, that she was distracting Joseph. Yes, he depended on Candy, but he belatedly recognized the need for a successor. Too late. I was bound for university in the fall, while Hoss, two years out of school, had left the auction world long behind. He drifted from job to job, taking on anything that demanded gloves to protect his hands. Nothing stuck. Like those losers in *Goin' Down the Road*, he threw out junk mail flyers instead of troubling to deliver them. In his new job, he tossed dynamite-shaped bundles of trees over the fence instead of planting them. He rested his aching back in bed, toking to early Genesis in headphones while I typed up an essay. He never recovered from the release of the band's *Abacab* album. Having discovered prog rock after its best-before date, Hoss was increasingly morose that its peak years had passed him by. It was impossible to find a piece longer than eight minutes, and there were no concept albums in sight. Yes reunited, but they went commercial. Jethro Tull went techno with Ian Anderson's flute buried under a million samples. Only the polyrhythmic sounds of the reformed King Crimson expanded the progressive vocabulary, and rumour had it they were breaking up again. Nothing stayed the same.

CANDY'S TELEGRAPHIC NOTE on the blackboard — "Rx. Later" — was nothing unusual, except she usually just wrote "R." It was only as the auction neared that we discovered she had not been at Rox's house that day. I peeked into Candy's bedroom, half-hoping to find her silently choosing a persona for the evening performance. There was no scowl to shoo me away, no fingers pushing against my back, no slammed door in my face.

Alone on the stage for the first time in years, Joseph tripped over words. He lowered the price rather than driving it up. He missed the most blatant signals for bids from patrons.

Auction-goers, so used to Candy's presence to liven up the endless parade of appliances, tools, and furniture, left early.

Well-versed in protocol from *The Rockford Files* and *Cannon*, Joseph waited twenty-four hours before contacting police to report Candy missing. He didn't believe she was gone. Joseph and I sat in front of the Predicta, feigning calm while ready to pounce on the telephone and the mailbox for news. All we got was an update from Hoss, who was in England in search of the lost chord of prog rock. Like Peter Gabriel, he wanted to feel his heart go boom-boom-boom. Except he'd confused Solsbury Hill with Salisbury Plain, and ended up at Stonehenge. I wanted news of Candy, and all I got was a bunch of rocks.

A week into her disappearance, all semblance of my inner calm was shattered. Payback for an entire year of thinking I had a life of my own. Joseph buried himself in work, but I quit my summer job as a lifeguard before it began. To hell with all those kids. If anyone needed saving, it was Candy.

I bought a staple gun for hydro poles, thumbtacks for community billboards in grocery stores, and cellophane tape for bathroom walls and stalls. Wearing a makeshift holster, I walked the streets with a grim countenance, thin-lipped, ready to draw my gun quickly. I affixed my *Missing Sister* poster to attract the best walk-by traffic, plastering my crisp, brightly coloured paper over the wrinkled and faded appeals for long-lost pets. I wanted to believe my efforts were hardly worth the trouble, that I would be blessed with a briefly lost sister. Taking a cue from the descriptions of beloved family dogs, I wrote under Candy's photo in block letters: *Does not answer when called.* No, Candy was loyal to no master or mistress except her artistic vision as Joseph's star assistant; apparently, she has thrown that away.

I read once that a dog leashed outside a store feels abandoned, no matter how many times its owner returns a few minutes later. I felt that sickness in my gut every time I entered a store to find no one had pulled off a tag with my name and number. When Candy was not waiting outside for me, my inner knots pulled tighter. I jumped when the telephone rang. If the technology had been available, I should have insisted on an implant under Candy's skin or set up an invisible security fence.

It all happened in June, two months before I left for university in Ottawa. Every morning I drove through surrounding villages to add more posters. These were bigger places, with two intersections and maybe a service station-cum-convenience store where a clergyman or gas jockey would notice a silent stranger. Afternoons, I checked the post office for responses to my classified ad offering a reward, and then scoured social notices in community newspapers for *Candy Grant, daughter of Joseph and the late Mary Grant, left home silently, but sends word she is fine and will return at a propitious moment.*

Evenings, I called Rox, who had a summer job dishing up hard ice cream in Spencerville, an ideal venue to gather intelligence on Candy. Our conversations were laced with tension from a mutual refusal to ask what we wanted to know. Her days were measured by how many kids inadvertently dislodged the top scoop with their tongues, sending it hurtling to the ground. She has a soft heart, and replaced the splattered ice cream on the sidewalk against the boss's orders, blaming herself for not sufficiently securing the Tiger Stripes and Rocky Roads. Some kids wallowed in their misery even after the source of the pain had been removed. Recounting these incidents turned her voice licorice black, and I wiped the receiver on my shirt before it short-circuited from my sweat and her spittle.

She liked to end the call with something funny that happened. I would hang up, dissatisfied but relieved she hadn't told me something I was unable to hear. In her three-inch heels, her loose Flapper-style skirt, and rouge applied liberally to both bare knees, Candy waited in line today behind whiny kids and short-tempered fathers with bellies protruding from vulgar T-shirts. She changed her mind at the counter, and while the rest of the customers sweated in the still humid air, a gentle breeze followed Candy, swishing her skirt as she sauntered off. I lay awake with these troubling fantasies, trying to push them aside with positive scenarios as sleep overtook me. Often I awoke, convinced that Candy was back, and it took a few blinks to separate fantasy from reality.

15

AMONG THE RUINS OF TINTAGEL Castle, ruminating on Rick Wakeman's musical interpretation of King Arthur, Hoss met a cranial sacral therapist who introduced him to the pastoral sounds of an ex-Genesis guitarist. Lying on the massage table, endorphins released from the gentle pressure on his skull and then caressed by elegiac minor chords that conjure up wandering minstrels, Hoss got immediate, if short-lived, relief to his hands.

Back in the new world, he had barely touched down in the Wasteland before announcing his move out west. In Nelson, British Columbia, he planned to learn the art of hands-on healing while indulging in free-ranging pot. On August evenings, after another fruitless search of our environs, I watched silently as Hoss painstakingly transferred his prog LPs onto more portable cassettes. It was a delicate operation, not one to be disrupted by a pointless recap of where I hadn't seen Candy.

For Hoss, our sister simply wised up to the constraints of small-town Ontario, and sought out a bigger canvas. Her disappearance was a sign of personal growth that should be celebrated. No doubt we would hear from her when she made good. Headlines. Reviews. Hoss told me all this while carefully folding his *A Friend with Weed Is a Friend Indeed* T-shirt into his backpack. On the eve of his departure, when he was almost out the door, I reached out desperately to hold him a half hour longer. But he had no time for a rerun of *Taxi*. His future awaited. Before bed, for consolation, I played his favourite Yes album — *Close to the Edge* — and pretended he was about to fall stoned off his bed in the dark. If I moved quickly, I could catch him.

It took all summer for me to see that maybe Hoss was right. Candy did not disappear to build a new life for herself in surrounding towns. She was after brighter lights. New York was too dramatic a leap. No one cared if you made it in Ottawa, but I was sure that was her first step. My four years in film studies gave me ample time to pick up her trail. I started spreading the news on campus and downtown, and then moved farther afield. No suburban neighbourhood was too upscale or skuzzy for my penetrating gaze and trusty staple gun. I staked out speech therapists, vintage clothing stores, my survey course on early cinema, anywhere that might have drawn Candy into the open.

Some of the Missing Sister posters in laundromats got marked up with moustaches, glasses, beards, eye patches. Exactly the way Candy would have laid waste to the cover of the weekly television guide to piss off Hoss. She was either sending me an encouraging sign or making herself more difficult to find. Apparently I had to earn the right to see her again through dogged pursuit. Lieutenant Gerard chasing Richard Kimble on *The Fugitive* did not have it this tough.

CANDY'S ABSENCE DREW larger crowds to the auctions. Some expected her to turn up, and wanted to be there for the big moment. I was one of them, sneaking down for Sunday evening auctions without telling Joseph. He had barely recovered his composure. Increasingly he lost control, conjuring up the Tone without warning. An edge of lament crept into his stream of words, an ache reminiscent of the *saudade* in Portuguese *Fado* songs. Faced with this projection of overwhelming longing for that which they'd never experienced, dealers who had thoroughly checked the box of *Sorry* in the preview now sensed the game was incomplete. As Joseph pitched jigsaw puzzles of the *Priaia de Marinha* in Portugal, older gentlemen who once took it on faith that no pieces were missing harboured doubts. They could not bear to recreate the scenes only to find holes in the boats or a broken sky. Soon they stopped coming altogether.

Those who showed up were increasingly indifferent. Joseph's chant filled entirely with nonsense words. He drifted off for minutes at a time without touching down, losing track of the latest bid. Far from gently insistent and cajoling, his tone became self-questioning, self-mocking. Really, it seemed to say, who would give me five dollars for this?

One evening I hid in the barn to see how Joseph fared when the patrons left. At midnight, he set out through the field for the flat rock. He walked with singular purpose, paying no attention to the quicksand pits. I moved to the stage, transfixed by a mournful chant pouring into the heavens, a Tone that made the clouds part and a bright star appear. I crumbled to my knees, convinced I saw Mary materializing among the shadows beyond the rock. Or was it Candy? I wasn't sure who Joseph was summoning, or who I wanted to see more.

Despite his passion for the mystical creatures that populated the prog-rock universe, and his fascination with auras and energy, Hoss had no patience for my reported sightings in the Wasteland. Living out west made his detachment from all things Candy all the easier. He urged me to say goodbye to the past, to accept facts, to embrace change. His new girlfriend was into Wicca, and could arrange a pagan blessing. We would stand in a circle where we faced the four directions with objects to represent earth, fire, air, and water. Place a photo of Candy on the altar, and call the elements to watch over us as we recite the incantations. More words. Maybe Candy left because we talked too much. Fending us off in the same house was no longer enough. Disappearance was the only choice, a natural extension of her silence.

Joseph stopped caring for his throat. Without hot tea and honey, it was often hoarse and ragged. He developed a persistent, hacking cough. I wondered if he screamed himself to sleep, alone in that house in the middle of nowhere, surrounded by dead land and live ghosts. Or was it the land that was alive, and Joseph who was becoming a ghost?

I CAME HOME the summer after my first year of university to help out with the auctions. Not to stand on the stage — no one could replace Candy — but to resume my childhood role as a lightning rod for grieving widows. Everyone knew our family history. Cradled by Joseph's soothing voice and the tender echo of our misfortunes, these widows momentarily forgot their own losses. I came to see us as performing a valuable public service. Joseph himself teared up at how they identified with him. As he spoke about how life throws us for a loop, his voice quaked with ever-more emotion. My presence on these sales trips was too much for Joseph, reminding him about what had been taken and what he'd failed to cultivate in me. Instead, I made my old rounds through the neighbouring villages in case Candy had tired of the nation's capital.

From Candy's desk, which overlooks the Wasteland, I could hear Joseph wander around in the dark on the dead soil. In the same way a stroke causes some people to adopt foreign accents, the trauma of Candy's disappearance caused Joseph to chant words from forgotten tongues. I heard the stamps and snorts of the neighbour's horses, how they were drawn to the strange sounds. But it was the wind — a fierce, relentless wind — that chilled my blood. Each tone Joseph produced churned up another gust, which rattled the open window and blew Candy's old papers on the floor. The house itself started to shake. Then silence.

I ran out back, behind the stage. The wind calmed. It was quiet. At the edge of the field, I peered into the darkness, childhood warnings rooting me in place. Joseph emerged a few yards to my left, humming, oblivious. For a second, as he passed under the light from the house, his face radiated inner contentment. Did I smell Tareyton cigarettes in the breeze? Or was that Candy on the rock, about to walk backwards again into our lives?

Molly O
The seductive cinema of Mickey Nailand

Home	Films	Suppositions	About Me

Backwards Walking
Posted by LJ

Each of Molly O's films with Mickey Nailand has a signature
moment where she is alone in a room: she undresses with
her back to the camera, but stops abruptly, as if she senses
someone watching. Finding no one, she continues, peeling off
outer clothes until she stands in underwear and bra. Again
she stops, but this time she "discovers" the camera. In the
hands of a lesser director, the woman would collude with the
audience, and begin a coy striptease. With Nailand, we get an
icily defiant stare from the woman — a look that belittles us
for watching. But the camera does not turn away. A battle of
wills ensues: who will blink first? Molly O takes an aggressive
stance, walking towards the camera, creating an extreme
close-up that blurs her features. Whenever the camera tries
to turn or pull back, she matches its moves. Then, her point
proven, she comes into focus — not through the director's
manipulation of the camera, but rather through her stepping

backwards into the room. She continues walking backwards, her gaze fixed on the camera, until she disappears through an open door behind her. Her ability to walk so effortlessly, so gracefully, without looking behind, reinforces just how firmly she remains in control of her body.

Leave a comment

16

THE FIRST TIME I SAW Candy walk backwards was in her bedroom. She enlisted me — through a series of hand gestures — to help rearrange her furniture. This was about six months before Hoss fell off the stage, stoned, so she must have been almost ten years old. In the north corner, newly uncovered, we put her desk. These were the original floors — hardwood, full of knots, warping and protruding with age. We pushed and pulled at it to make it flat, and a board came loose. We sat quite still, staring at the hole in the floor we uncovered. I was taken with a heavy sense of guilt. To make things right, I put the wood back in place. It fell through the hole. Quickly, I reached into the dark space to pull it out again, and my fingers brushed against something. Candy stood up, shaking, and walked backwards — desperately trying to distance herself from the discovery, but unable to take her eyes off it. With her room in disarray, she bumped into her bed and fell backwards on the mattress. She was near tears — not from physical hurt, but out of fear.

A lock of brown hair, a thin, unframed daguerreotype, and a note. The strands of hair in Candy's palm were funnel-shaped, like a cartoon tornado. She poked at them cautiously with her index finger. When they didn't bite, she stroked them gently, with affection. I was the one who opened the folded paper, and tried to read the faint markings in pencil. They were too faded to decipher. The image in the picture, however, was clear: a young girl — curly dark hair, serious, possibly sad. In ink, etched on the metal, a single name: Phebe.

Candy overcame all her fears. She held the image — it is perhaps two inches square — between two fingers, and studied the girl closely. Her lips moved as if she could make out the words in the note, and I was torn between eyeing the paper and lip-reading to understand what she saw. I only knew she wrapped it all up again, stuck it in the hole, and had me reinstall the dislodged board. She pointed to me, then her, and then brought a finger to her lips. It warmed me inside, this half-secret that we shared.

It was Hoss who put the idea in my head that Isaac, Lewis, and Phebe were watching us. He said Lewis would smite me in my bed, cut off my toes to stunt my growth. I wore socks that night, and stayed awake to see if they had been sliced open. I believed Hoss until I saw him carving his height with a knife in the barn, so frustrated that at age ten I have grown taller. Never mind he will spurt past me again in four months, or that his blue eyes are 20/20. I was wearing glasses by sixth grade. I don't know about Candy's green eyes. Maybe she was blind and never told us.

WHEN CANDY DISAPPEARED, I went straight to the hiding place, sure she'd left a note. I pulled out Phebe's time capsule, and studied it anew for clues. Because of their shared birthday, and this secret message from the past, Candy had every reason to identify with Phebe — much more so than Hoss and I had with Isaac and Lewis. If Candy were somehow re-enacting Phebe's disappearance, it made sense she, too, would have left a cache for the future hidden behind another loose board. I spent many weeks in the house and the barn, pulling, pushing, tapping, and prying everything in sight. I told no one since this would mean coming clean about Phebe's time capsule. I could not betray Candy's trust. My knuckles were raw, my spirit dampened.

I held Phebe's note close to the lamp in case she wrote it in lemon juice. I studied the lines with a magnifying glass, trying to see what Candy saw. I read Candy's school notebooks, searching for clues in the margins — secret messages passed between her and Rox during class. Nothing.

Maybe there weren't any words on Phebe's note. Not any more. Time had erased them. It was this absence that frightened Candy, the knowledge that Phebe's life was reduced to a single photograph and a few strands of hair. Whatever thoughts and feelings she wanted to share with the future have vanished. It was a leap of faith, this time capsule, and it failed. Perhaps Candy learned from Phebe. No reliance on words, written or spoken. Only her work with Mickey Nailand would be her legacy. An audacious bet with fate that her genius would one day be discovered and appreciated. She became a recluse like Greta Garbo to preserve and foment the mystery, freezing the allure in place. When the time comes the world will know, and not know, Molly O. All she needs is one person to bring her back to life. Such a diabolical plan. Who is crazier? Candy for dreaming it up or me for making it come true? I am so cool with the programmers at Anthology Film Archives. When someone jokes that a Nailand retrospective may draw Molly O out of the woodwork, I turn my eyes from the webcam lest they reveal my true agenda.

The only hint that Phebe has left any mark at all on Candy: a history essay called "A Stitch in Time" in which she argued that alphabet samplers not only allowed pioneer girls to overcome the drudgery of their lives through arts and crafts, they also permitted the creation of a feminine space that was both public and private. Within the constraints of the form, girls developed distinct styles, and yet colluded in the stitching of fanciful capital letters to mock the virtuous messages they were required to reproduce. Their signatures — imposed by proud parents to show off their daughters — were seen by the girls as a way to become part of history. The survival of the samplers showed the girls were right. In giving her a D+, her male teacher wrote simply: *How do you know this?*

THE HUM OF the microwave provides the soundtrack as I check my blog for comments. I take my Hungry Man Dinner onto the back stoop, the better to sense old vibrations from Candy and Rox. The tray grows cold on my lap as I listen to the crickets, feel the cool breeze, gaze at the stars hovering over the dead field. In a *Peanuts* cartoon, Charlie Brown sits on his front step, waiting for friends to call instead of calling on them. Night falls. A wasted day.

On the desk, beside the laptop, lie Joseph's draft memoirs. All my offers to help him organize his thoughts, and all his objections and reassurances amount to this: a handwritten page with a single line at the top: *Backwards Walking — Reminiscences of a Country Auctioneer.* No table of contents, no outline, not a single hint of the trajectory. I hold the page up to the lamp in case heat will reveal any hidden letters.

Of course the title strikes me as less about Joseph looking back at his life than about Candy's signature move. Walking freely between the three tiers of the stage in her various costumes, holding, and pointing at objects of desire, Candy learned quickly not to turn her back to the crowd. Instead of showcasing her behind, she walked backwards with astonishing ease, always in character, always sensing the edge, never tripping. She sashayed, targeting any man watching her. Caught in the act, even the most self-confident men dropped their eyes to the ground. At no time did she give up control. Even Joseph — the only one behind her — delayed the start of the next round of bidding until Candy was in position. She toyed with him some evenings, adjusting buttons in her Dietrich tails or tucking in loose threads for her Garbo dress. He tolerated these antics, knowing she was the star but never imagining she could soon be a star for someone else.

Molly O
The seductive cinema of Mickey Nailand

| Home | Films | Suppositions | About Me |

A Stitch in Time
Posted by LJ

Mickey Nailand had a congenital heart condition that, combined with his artistic temperament, was enough to close the books on his death. It also helped explain his intense working rhythm. He knew time was short.

The romantics speculate that Nailand's death shook Molly O so much that she took her own life. How else could she have so thoroughly vanished from the public eye? I think Molly O is shrewd, disappearing to cultivate mystery through her absence. And I also believe the time has come for Molly O to step forward and take credit for her unsung role as an equal creative partner in Nailand's artistic project. Indeed, I argue the films, as a whole, can be understood as a documentary on the personal and creative relationship between Mickey Nailand and Molly O.

In the original eleven-minute version of *The Slave* (1909), for example, Pickford plays the wife of a struggling artist who sells herself to help the family make ends meet. In an early draft of the new script, clearly influenced by Sirk and Fassbinder, Nailand amplifies the melodrama to comment on the wife's noble sacrifice and depicts a conventional parade of lovers. Nailand typed out four more scripts, each giving the wife more and more power. In the final filmed version, the Greek sculptor, played by Nailand, becomes an Italian silent-era filmmaker who insists his wife, Molly O, pose for lucrative naughty films. Under the camera's glare, the mousy wife transforms into a tigress. Not only does the experience liberate her sexually, it turns her into a cunning businesswoman who makes them fabulously wealthy.

The formal construction of the scenes is telling. In the fictional story, the wife appears increasingly in control, toying with the belt to show her husband just who is wearing the pants in the family. Yet she is still the object of the camera's gaze. To challenge that gaze, she moves in and out of the frame; she approaches the lens until her bare skin blurs into nothingness; she drops to her knees or turns her back. In other words, the wife determines what we see.

The camera tries to match and even anticipate her moves, as far as the tripod will allow, until the wife seizes the camera and films her husband running out the door. The closed door is shot for five minutes, this time with a sometimes jerky handheld camera. But since there are no edits in this long sequence, we can never lose sight of the fact that, behind the camera, stands a naked woman. A naked woman who, despite everything that's happened, we still hope to see emerge.

This sequence creates a new language of erotica. Throughout the struggle between the husband and wife, her bare skin flashes for a few seconds at a time. With no conventional titillation, the film nevertheless instills a sense of longing in the viewer. The use of the handheld also creates a sense of anticipation: never has the shot of a door been so erotically charged.

Here is the question: how much of this struggle is between the characters in the story, and how much between Nailand and Molly O? Was Molly O forcing changes to the script? Were the two struggling in the editing room as well?

This was only their third film together, and it foreshadows the creative tensions ahead. In the last scenes of the film, the wife challenges her husband's artistic decisions, which brings about their downfall. Perhaps Nailand thought Molly O would either make them wealthy or cause their financial ruin. Certainly, no one got rich from their films, which have languished, undistributed, and generally unscreened, at the Co-op since his death. Yet there are also scripts, production notes, still photos. Molly O knew enough to protect their legacy. Instead of hiding a time capsule under floorboards, she made sure the work would be found, lest it fade away.

Leave a comment

17

I WONDER IF MY BLOG should be less directed to film aficionados and more targeted to the only reader I care about. All I want is to connect the dots. But I don't think an open-hearted pitch would appeal to Candy. I have to stay oblique, and give her the pleasure of decoding my references.

What would happen if I did stumble across Candy at a red light? Would I jump out in the middle of the street, abandon my car, and slide in beside her? No, it would feel too forced. An unwelcome triumph of my will. Despite my hopes and dreams of running into Candy around the next corner, I want her to find me. At times I must sound like a crazed ex-lover, not a sibling. This worries me. In *Pierrot le Fou*, Marianne's boyfriend turns out to be her brother. But I fear turning into Pierrot — someone who paints his face blue and then accidentally blows himself up.

No scanning images, videos, and text links. No searches of dating sites, archives, or court records. No payment to private investigators. Only a blog that drops hints of our child-hood, that flatters her artistic ego and mine, enticing her to overcome decades of silence and mystery. Even with no comments registered, I have to believe she has discovered it. Rather than announce her return with cheap talk on a screen, she will make a grand entrance on her own terms. There is no reason to think this. It's my leap of faith.

I have less confidence that Hoss will check his voicemail after his island retreat. His recharged energetic antennae may not pick up on Joseph's passing or maybe the battery in his mobile is drained. Never has the Wasteland seemed so vacant. If I could find an old Tareyton cigarette, I would watch smoke rise in familiar shapes to the ceiling, and feel less alone. A pathetic reverie, but I know I'm right.

JOSEPH'S SIXTY VHS tapes of *All My Children* are neatly labelled with the airdate and a few key words about plots involving the identical twins portrayed by David Canary. I watch back-to-back episodes until two in the morning, totally taken by the tactics of ruthless businessman Adam and his brother Stuart, the nice-guy artist, in the suburb of Pine Valley, Pennsylvania.

Hoss is the bad son, the ingrate first-born who refuses to carry on the family tradition, the one hooked on demon weed who abandons us after Candy disappears. Joseph never fails to criticize Hoss's flaky profession, and I defend my brother, although in my secret self I'm more critical than Joseph. Part of me is still twelve years old, wanting everyone to get along.

I am the good lad, loved by default since I take up so little space and ruffle so few feathers. I am the dunce with the foolscap proudly writing down high bids, the desperate apprentice whose heart breaks along with his voice from being ignored, the willing accomplice on Joseph's excursions to manipulate the hearts of widows. If I strayed from the roles I willingly took on, his love would have slipped away, swallowed by quicksand. And I would jump in right after, or so I promise myself. The perfect accomplice to everyone who needs me, including me.

I watch infomercials until three, mourning the loss of the four-channel universe and the sheer unpredictability of the Predicta's basic functions. It stands in the corner, unused but still taking up space. An object from the past Joseph is unable to cast aside. I miss Hoss picking the shows, Candy studying the fashions in black and white, and me taking it all in.

THE DAISY SHEETS Candy likes so much are limp and stale after decades in the closet, nothing like the everlasting freshness we brag about in our make-believe commercials. I give them a shot of Febreze before making up the bed.

All traces of chocolate from Jos. Louis cakes in my bed are long gone. Hoss would return late with the munchies from a weed-n-feed night in Shep, his serenity replaced with an itch to share tales of laid-back sex in the car. I leave the sheets in a crumpled heap directly underneath the black stain of smoke in the ceiling. No point in making up the bed. I believe less and less he will show.

This is the brother who would sit stoned on the bed, look at me profoundly, and say, "I think it's time for 'Supper's Ready.'" I would close our bedroom door so Hoss could crank up the volume and I could hide from Candy. All right for her to wear dainty lace wrist warmers on the auction stage, but I feared her ridicule at the sight of me in white latex gloves, complicit in our brother's solemn rituals. Hoss would remove the LP from the plastic sleeve of *Foxtrot* with great ceremony, and place it on the turntable. I would squeeze a few drops of special cleanser into his state-of-the-art Discwasher system, and brush invisible particles from the vinyl for two revolutions. He couldn't trust his own hands so I was tasked to blow any remaining dust from the stylus, and lower it in the right groove. Then I would try to hear the deep truths he could hear, tolerating his habitual lament that without Peter Gabriel the band had lost its progressive edge. Hoss would still be sailing among the gutterflies and flutterbyes as I carefully and quietly re-inserted the record into its slip and cover. I would return the album to its designated spot in the Genesis section with the attention of an archivist handling an illuminated manuscript.

All these years his prog records have been sitting here in milk crates, souring. It leaves a bad taste in my mouth, the hours wasted serving Hoss on a platter. Not to mention the time spent spying on Candy, and teaching Rox to edit in the barn. Where were my dreams in all this? It's only now I have them, and they still don't feel mine.

I HAVE KEPT all Hoss's cards, letters, and emails, and all his gifts of books with words like *soul*, *essence*, and *unity* in the titles. I haven't read them, just as he probably hasn't watched the Stephen Dwoskin films I've sent him. Mostly we stick to safe territory like the release of old shows on DVD and his *saudade* for mediocre movies-of-the-week from the 1970s that could have made interesting TV series like *Sheila Levine Is Dead and Living in New York* and *Girl in the Empty Grave*. He envisions intricate storylines for the first seasons of these stillborn dramas. All these girls who aren't quite dead can't be a coincidence. On some unconscious level that his therapies have not yet excavated, Hoss believes Candy is out there, waiting for the right script. At least I hope so, since this will make him more receptive to my discovery of Molly O.

I have my own what-if scenarios. If Mary had survived labour, she and Candy would have grown together, experiencing all the usual envy, distrust, and rage of normal mothers and adolescent daughters. Or they would have fed each other's unique brand of silence. Mary, after all, was only quiet and reserved, not mute. A daughter like Candy might have pushed her over the edge. Equally plausible, she would have prevented Joseph from using her as bait for auction-goers. Then again, Candy would have rebelled against our mother's protection, made things worse that much sooner. And me? What if I had not been so pathologically determined for Candy to fill up the space left by our mother? My sister was a sensitive creature who could easily have picked up on these projections. What if I had never kept the Steenbeck or manipulated Candy into joining the cinema club? What if my desire to be close is what drove her away? What if this is more grandiosity, a fantasy that whatever I do makes a difference?

I like to think that Candy rebelled against Mickey Nailand, his insistence they move from New York City upstate to West Saugerties. Did he really think to soak up the vibes of Dylan and The Band after all this time? Small-town living is maybe why Candy fled us, after all — the endless fields, the boredom, the lack of culture. Maybe she just threatened to leave, which pushed Nailand over the edge. I know it would have done me in; but the truth is, the move may have been Candy's idea. She may well be there now, selling wild flowers in the village square, printing poems on a handmade press, holding a pose for a life drawing class. I can write a thousand storylines, each richer and more detailed than the last, all filtered through my own dreams, desires, and hang-ups. This endless mental masturbation is what keeps me going. An agonizing pleasure, this never being sure, this never being released.

18

THE FIXED LENS IN ROX'S camera frames her face between the eyebrows and neck. The covers are pulled up tightly and no doubt she's crawled into bed fully clothed in four layers — not to deal with changes in temperature, but to thwart unwanted sexual attention.

She only Skypes when we're both in my Montreal condo, on opposite sides of the wall. We talk virtually until she falls asleep; but she often wakes suddenly, worry lines tightening in confusion until she sees me on the screen. In a few hours, the battery in her mobile will be dead and the connection lost. Until then, she fades in and out of consciousness, long periods of silence interrupted by a rumbling laugh that jerks my hand off the mouse and rolls my chair backwards. She won't calm down until I fall out of bed, the way I did when we were kids. I bang plastic hand weights against the wall to create the satisfying thud her unconscious craves.

She shows up without notice, so I have taken to sleeping on the couch in the office, giving her the bedroom, just in case. At times I try to decide if the ripples and curves of the comforter hide human form. She blends into the landscape, perfectly camouflaged. I swear my bed is empty, only to find her fixing breakfast in the morning.

Since she spooks easily, I have installed three deadbolts on the front door and left the hardwood floors bare and squeaky. I peck at the keyboard when she's around; the clicking keys make her think someone's picking the lock. I would have been happy with a somber, ground-floor rental. No hauling groceries and my bicycle up winding stairs. But Rox has been visibly relaxed in the bright space on the second floor, so I have no regrets about buying.

In these years of her intermittent squatting, we haven't so much as hugged or air kissed. We eat our own popcorn. We separate the laundry by gender, as well as colour. Neither of us evokes the ring-around-the-collar reenactments, how she usurped me as the narrator belittled by Candy's unrepentant housewife. Our mixed feelings remain unsorted.

We do not speak of Candy's disappearance, yet she is the bond between us, our shared unspoken history. What secrets Rox is protecting, I don't know. I'm just glad she comes around, and resent when she doesn't. There is always the chance she will bring news of Candy, and I am invariably crushed and relieved by the silence between us. It's all I can do not to deliver handmade, gold-embossed invitations on bended knee. *I entreat you, Rox, to reveal all you know about Candy's current whereabouts.* The blank look of despair on her face would be too much to bear.

It's easier to be close when she is not here. The mixed tapes she sends, with hand-drawn covers, are treasures, even as the format grows increasingly anachronistic. I read into Annette Peacock songs like "So Close Is Still Too Far," "Safe Inside the Fantasy," and "No Winning, No Losing," convinced Rox is transmitting a message. What, I don't know.

The first time she arrives at my door, I don't recognize her. Her body and voice are too thin. I don't ask, simply offer my couch. She hibernates, fattens up, disappears. Every winter is the same. No questions, no answers. The unexpected arrivals in the shoulder seasons. She works in Montreal when she's here. Or at least she disappears most days, and buys vintage clothes from the *friperies*. Some of her dresses could be Candy's costumes. We both know it. There's no reason to express it aloud.

I don't ask about her love life, nor does she about mine. For me, the height of the sexual act brings a moment of addictive forgetfulness. But I can't bask in this state for long, and the awakening is rude. I can fake connection curled up against my lovers, but my inattention to their words gets me into trouble. Only so many times can I get by with "Hmm hmm" before they ask a question that requires a more thoughtful response. The confession that I haven't really been listening at all, the hurt feelings, the tears, and even the reconciliation, all wear me out. I prefer the platonic silence between me and Rox, even if, at times, it weighs heavily. All those nights in my bed. Sometimes I have unnatural thoughts. She is like a sister to me. I stuff the feelings before they grow. Who am I fooling? I don't know if Rox feels the same. To speak these thoughts aloud would betray, or at least water down, the purity of my preoccupation with Candy.

These past few months have seen regular and longer visits, and I have been tempted to share my discovery of Molly O, to invite her to help edit the collage from the Molly O films or to read my blogs. Except that I'm convinced Rox knows about Molly O already. It's not possible that Candy could have disappeared without telling her best friend. All these years Rox has guarded her secret, respecting Candy's desire for privacy, occasionally teasing and tormenting me. So it seems, at least.

Scenario one: I'm screening *Diary of a Lost Girl*, a Louise Brooks film I discovered in high school, when two figures slip into my dark classroom. I recognize the shape of Rox's flounced flamenco dress and bohemian shawl, which shields her short companion from view. They sit discreetly at the back, as if they rejoined the film club. I break my own rule, switching the lights on early, while the credits are rolling, but both are gone. Only a pair of white satin gloves on the floor hints at Candy's fleeting presence.

All that evening, I wait for Rox to show up triumphantly with Candy. Then for days and weeks after. Doubts set in. I set the gloves on the kitchen table with the subtlety of product placement. Two months pass before I wake to find Rox writing in her journal at the kitchen table. No reaction to my dropped hints about diaries or glances at the gloves within her reach. I start to question whether Candy has the audacity to make a cameo appearance in my classroom. In *Public Enemies*, Johnny Depp as Dillinger walks brazenly into a police station and passes unnoticed; but, as Rox prepares breakfast, I'm thinking more of *Public Enemy*, how Cagney shoves half a grapefruit into his lover's face at the breakfast table. Sure I'm angry. At whom is not so clear.

Never before has Rox Skyped me when I'm not on the other side of the bedroom wall. It must mean something. The lost girl could be sitting at the kitchen table right now, fingering her gloves.

Molly O
The seductive cinema of Mickey Nailand

| Home | Films | Suppositions | About Me |

Hand in glove
Posted by LJ

Molly O is never entirely naked. She may be exposed or
paraded on screen — either obscured or so fully frontal her
parts are distorted — and her body may be contorted into all
manner of sexual positions, but her hands are always covered.
Even more interesting: she only wears gloves in the sex scenes.
In what amounts to a jump cut, the gloves suddenly appear
on her hands as soon as her clothes are off.

It's no accident or mistake: it happens in every sex scene in
Nailand's oeuvre. Is it fetishism or prudery? No, the regular
appearance of the white gloves illustrates the creative tension
between Nailand and Molly O, and how the actress is truly in
control. The glove is a sheath, in more ways than one.

In the original *M'liss*, a plucky young girl in a rough-and-
tumble mining camp falls in love with her teacher, helping
him escape a mob that wants to lynch him for a murder he

did not commit. In Nailand's remake, a black teacher seduces a thirteen-year-old white student, Molly O, who seems remarkably experienced for her age. They meet after school for several weeks until the secret is out. The girl's enraged father pounds on the school door; and, with a posse of self-righteous white folks, lynches the teacher in the yard next to the play structure.

In each of the sex scenes, the teacher watches Molly O undress. Stein has argued persuasively that the act of striptease is, in fact, homoerotic: the woman's body signifies the phallus, and men are watching the clothes drop to see it revealed. Nailand makes this connection literal: he intercuts the teacher putting on a condom with the girl inserting her fingers into satin gloves. After sex, the teacher carefully discards the condom, while the girl throws her sheaths off with abandon, much like Rita Hayworth strips off and throws her glove after singing "Put the Blame on Mame" in *Gilda*.

Gilda, of course, is slapped in the face for stepping outside the bounds of propriety. It seems that a woman's sexuality must be controlled at all costs, but nothing can contain Molly O. For her, the gloves are a way to retain power in unbalanced relationships. Never will she allow her guard down: her body sheathed, her soul armoured. If she lets go, it will be on her own terms.

In the final scene, the girl's father spanks her bare behind. The title card: "This hurts me more than it hurts you." Her apparent indifference enrages him all the more. He shakes his sore hand. Yes, finally, his actions did hurt him more. *Amarilly of Clothes-Line Alley* offers an even more complex take on the power struggle between director and actress, and deserves as much notoriety as Jacques Rivette's *La Belle Noiseuse*, released a year later, in 1991.

Leave a comment

19

UNDER ROX'S INTENSE STARE — RIGHT into the lens of her iPhone camera — the news about Joseph's death remains unspoken. My eyes stray to the bulletin board on my wall and the notice for *Pandora's Box* at the high school film club. Not for the first time do I wonder whether Louise Brooks's character Loulou is a prototype for Molly O. Both sow lust in the hearts of men and women, leading them to rash decisions.

Rox dozes off, and her iPhone slips a notch in her palm. The faintest white puffs of smoke have invaded her ebony hair. When did this happen? Truth is, I might be looking for the first time, which is still a better record than my own self-regard. I will pace the apartment with my toothbrush and cordless razor rather than face the mirror. It disturbs me too much, to take notice of the years that have passed.

The "Recent Publications" page of my website is gathering dust. My irreverent reviews and acerbic banter with the host of the afternoon radio drive-home show have long been archived on cassette tapes, a medium that none of the young bucks in the department seem to recognize. My classes devoted to early cinema and experimental filmmakers like Stephen Dwoskin have been displaced in popularity by the post-colonial and feminist concoctions of the new hires. Once my sabbatical ends, if I don't raise my profile, I may end up teaching Slasher Films 101 to earn my keep.

I don't talk to Rox about any of this, but her sudden appearances make it easier to handle all the same. While she is a tangible connection to Candy, I actually become less preoccupied with finding Candy when Rox is around. A day after one of Rox's equally abrupt departures, of course, I plunge into a dark hole, full of anxiety and guilt for time not spent obsessing about Candy. Where does Rox go when she disappears out my door? How does she spend her days? I imagine a series of friends with whom she squats, never so long to be a nuisance, always the perfect guest.

Rox has a cameo in *Going, going, gone.* She is editing images of Candy dressed as Marlene Dietrich in tails, unaware Candy has snuck into the barn with the Bolex. Frame by frame, the images are deconstructed, appear less and less real. Candy zooms in on the Marlene image on the screen, leaving Rox's shoulders and head slightly out of focus. It appears spontaneous. Yet nothing in film is accidental. Not like life. I could tell Rox I've got the film on my computer, along with the entire Molly O collection. It might ease us into speaking about painful subjects. Except her iPhone slips completely from her hands and she disappears from my view.

I wake on the floor, shoulder and knee sore to the touch. It's been decades since I've been driven out of bed at the Wasteland. There is only one explanation. Rox is here. She knows Candy is coming. They have been in contact through the years, just as I've believed. I'm shaking now — not from the vibrations but rather from the betrayal. Always the two of them pushing me to one side. Even now, after I've engineered this reunion, they are the stars and I am the voiceover. Not the omniscient, authoritarian, voice-of-doom style narrator I would prefer to be, but a fragmented, self-doubting author unspooling in a mess behind the projector.

I crawl into the hall on all fours. Scrambling to my feet, I'm thrown against the door by a muffled laugh from inside Candy's room. My sister's bed is made up, pillows fluffed, covers turned down — just the way I left it. Rox lies on the cot on the floor, just the way she did. The force of my body against the door has soothed her fears, sent her into a deep sleep. I make my way back to my room, determined to shut out her infectious laugh if it emerges again, knowing I'll crawl back instead.

Molly O
The seductive cinema of Mickey Nailand

| Home | Films | Suppositions | About Me |

Of blank slates and sham love
Posted by LJ

With the high-minded narrative strategies at work in Mickey Nailand's films, the uncomfortable use of the male gaze, the uneasy relationship between director and star, the tragedy of his early death and Molly O's vanishing trick, it's easy to overlook the one element that unites his work: humour, often relying for its effect on an appreciation of language and idiom.

In *Oh, Uncle,* as Molly O defends against the advances of Uncle John, the film's title is repeated with varying degrees of intent: disgust, boredom, embarrassment. The last title card, in an echo of the old schoolyard submission, can be read with a dreamy sigh: "Uncle!" This film also has the first of Nailand's visual puns: a scene where Molly O, wearing her French maid uniform, removes her panties and then "trips" in the dining room with the tea service, flying literally "ass over teakettle." As the uncle paddles her backside with a switch,

Molly O proclaims "Oh, I love slapstick!"

One Hundred Percent American is also full of visual puns. My favourite is the bondage scene where the auctioneer's daughter forces the draft dodger to tie her up, and makes him bid for sex — a perverse form of "liberty bond."

All this humour comes from the characters played by Molly O. The deadpan look of Nailand is more Buster Keaton than Fatty Arbuckle, whereas Molly O can conjure up the pithy look of Theda Bara or Louise Brooks at will. Whatever its source, the humour is double-edged, undercutting the eroticism.

In *Mrs. Jones Entertains*, Molly O plays a deaf-mute maid who helps her mistress prepare for a grand party in the mansion. She carries a small blackboard and chalk in her apron so she can communicate. Each time she prints her words on the blackboard, the inter-titles reproduce chalk-like block letters. A hand subsequently appears on the screen with a shammy to wipe off the words. Given this is a silent film, everyone is mute. When Molly O laughs, an inter-title appears with "Ha, Ha, Ha," as if it's not enough to see the expression on her face.

Molly O becomes the "mistress," drawing each of the male guests into the drawing room. Earlier she has been drawing erotic figures on the blackboard. With each new lover, she holds up the same claim on her chalkboard: "I'm a blank slate!" The hand with the shammy appears on the screen, makes a motion to wipe off the blackboard, then reconsiders.

Cut to Molly O, with her white glove, catching a shammy thrown from off-screen. She uses it to protect the furniture while she stimulates her lovers.

The gag is repeated four times, with the letters on the blackboard getting "rubbed off" more each time. This creates collusion between Molly O and the audience: we admire her cavalier attitude towards the men, how she can't be bothered to reprint the message; we enjoy recognizing the tension between her claims and how the words are represented figuratively and literally. Ultimately, "I'm a blank slate" becomes "I'm late." Late for freedom? By the end of the film, she has emptied the suit pockets of all her would-be suitors, and fled. The joke, finally, is on them.

Leave a comment

20

ON OUR SECOND GO-ROUND on Skype, Rox looks at me rather than the camera in her iPhone, which sends her gaze off-kilter — an attempt at intimacy that falls flat.

— I found Joseph in the field. The ambulance snuck up on me. No sirens. The way you do.

— He came to me last night in a dream.

— I think ...

— Can I finish my feelings, please? His voice bathed me in a warm light. I used to visit. My own house was so sterile. Joseph took an interest in my life. He had to ask me questions twice because I would lose myself in his voice. I stopped coming by. I don't know why. I felt the need to see him again. We wrote sometimes.

Rox wants forgiveness for keeping her visits to my father a secret or for ending them abruptly. All I can think is how Joseph never asked how I was doing. Maybe I should have gone to see Rox's parents. I want to keep Rox talking.

I don't want this moment to end.

— He used to watch this soap opera with twin brothers. You remember when we acted out laundry commercials.

— No, we never did. You and Candy, then me and Candy.

— We were always cleaning something. Something was always dirty. Did she ever tell you about Phebe?

— The girl ...

— ... who lived here. They shared a birthday. She left a message.

— The lock ...

— ... of hair, yes. And a message too faded to read. Did she ever tell you? Hoss is coming. Maybe.

— Does he ...

— I can't reach him.

— He's at ...

— ... a retreat, yes. On an island. Not far. With his Momentous Moments group. He says he'll come if the moment feels right.

— I think ...

— Joseph tore down the bus shelter. Why?

— How are you feeling, finding Joseph like that?

— How long will you stay?

We lose the connection. This is why I never ask. It makes her feel I don't want her around when the opposite is true.

COME DAWN, ROX and I will emerge from our separate rooms with the awkwardness of long-time penpals who finally meet in the flesh. In the light of day, our half-voiced intimacies from the night before will retreat into the shadows. At breakfast, she will stare into her dippy egg and trace parallel lines with her spoon on the vinyl placemat. I will offer toothpicks of buttered toast to pry open the unspoken truths about Candy that quiver on Rox's lips. If nothing emerges, I will speak of my discovery of Mickey Nailand, and gauge her reaction. She has already let slip her secret life with Joseph, and the moment is ripe for all she knows to pour out. Like the Jack Nicholson character in *A Few Good Men*, she is dying to divulge the truth about her transgression.

Do you or do you not know anything about Candy's disappearance?

You're goddamned right I do!

There'll be no accusations from me. I'll show her there's nothing more to be gained from silence, either for her or Candy. Tease her a little, and the pride Rox takes in her long subterfuge will spill out in fits of nervous laughter. Keep my hands free to catch the lighter dishes before the deep and jagged tremor in her voice pushes them off the edge of the table. I will bear her no malice, so relieved at having my theories confirmed. Rox may well know of Candy's reaction to my blog, and even her estimated time of arrival at the Wasteland. There is no telling what the morning may bring.

21

OUR LIPS REMAIN SEALED FROM habitual reticence and the congealing effects of the morning oatmeal. We make our way up the dusty road, bandanas covering our mouths and noses like outlaws from the Old West about to stick up a bank. Staring ahead at the vast frontier, Rox and I are hidden from sheriffs and deputies and even from ourselves. I am worried about missing Candy's arrival, back at the Wasteland. If I asked, maybe Rox would have reassuring words for me. But if she knows nothing, I will be no further ahead and my spirit will be crushed. So I don't share Mickey Nailand, Molly O, or the blog with her. We continue our dance of non-disclosure, and I wonder if she feels as I do — empowered and imprisoned by silence. There's something to be said for the comfort of inertia.

I've packed a bottle of mosquito repellant for the return journey, along with a flashlight. Right now there's enough light to sidestep the rocks that have sprung up overnight.

Unlikely there will be cars, but if the wind picks up it will cause a blinding sandstorm. I have thrown a couple of old windbreakers with the reflective decal "Bring Me Back Alive" into my knapsack and we will drape them over our shoulders, Batman-style, as they're too small to wear. Ridiculous, yes, but I no longer fear ridicule.

HOSS AND I wore our windbreakers the length of the driveway, then stashed them in the bus shelter. It was worth having them bring us back dead not to have safety decals clash with our costumes. The frisson of disobedience made me feel two years older.

There were only four houses on the road, spread over two miles, each with a driveway that took ten minutes to traverse. We trundled along with our plastic pumpkin containers, collecting our goodies, returning after two hours to empty our haul on the kitchen table. Rox's family gave out miniature bags of chips. The Sandersons, who had horses, gave out candy-flavoured necklaces or suckers. We never knew the names of the people in the last house, which had a real cemetery on the property. Every year they gave apples, which Joseph insisted we throw away for fear of needles, pins, and razor blades. While Hoss gave up on them after three Halloweens, I went back one last time, thinking that year it would be different. I was like Charlie Brown in his annual attempt to kick the football, convinced this was the year that Lucy wouldn't pull it away at the last second. I was dressed as a ghost, a single sheet draped over my head with holes cut for my eyes, nose, and mouth. With no peripheral vision, and my ears covered with the sheet, I could block out the cemetery. It was different that time. Instead of an apple, I got a rock.

Joseph sent us to take Candy around, when she was old enough. Despite her name, she only liked the dressing-up part. Of course she never yelled out "Trick or Treat," just stared down the neighbours until they dished out. Soon enough she ditched her brothers for Rox. Hoss was happy to see her go. Then he too went out with his friends. Pirate, ghoul, warlock, I was at heart a lone superhero, keeping a keen eye on the girls from the shadows.

THERE'S A PHOTOGRAPH of Candy lying on the roof of Rox's bus shelter, chin resting on her folded hands. The shack has been freshly painted, a base of green with a single white daisy on a stem flowering to the roof, just under Candy's face. It is the girls' handiwork, this shack, inside and out. Wild vines growing up the side and across the entrance have overtaken the painted stem. The daisy has faded, its petals fallen one by one. She loves me, she loves me not. Rox takes a small hatchet from her bag, and hacks away at the growth. With trepidation, I enter this private girls' space where who knows what went on. Even with the west-facing window, the interior is dark. Rox shoos away my flashlight, retrieving a candle and matches from her bag. She hands it to them, standing in the shadows while I examine the script on the walls. I half expect hieroglyphics or ancient runes, but find instead the clear and confident strokes of Candy's cursive. Here, not twenty minutes from the Wasteland, my sister has installed a time capsule in plain sight. Her words are not faded after years beneath pine floorboards, but are etched firmly in black ink on white walls — even if the nib of her thin marker occasionally bumped against the grain in the particle board. The wall I saved for her in our own shelter, apparently, wasn't good enough.

I long to discover emotional outbursts, explanations, getaway plans. Under the faint light of the candle, a shout-out of silent film actresses emerges, topped by Marlene Dietrich. It gives way to quotations from Virginia Woolf and Sylvia Plath, whose dark and acerbic moods are inscribed with a particularly heavy hand on the wall. This is Candy by proxy. Stand-ins and body doubles substituting for the real thing. I pour over the words, hoping to find her between thousands of swirling lines that snake through the letters. This insidious tangle of weeds seems determined to choke the life out of what Candy left behind. It leaves me gasping. Would someone in cahoots with my sister have carried out such a vengeful act? Rox has been in the dark all this time, as much as I have. Is this what she is trying to tell me? A lifetime of suffering and confusion, a heart rendered inert by rage and hurt, beating only to mark empty days. The thought is too much to bear. How will Rox react to the news that I've discovered Candy, that, through my blog, she will find her way home.

Rox and I return to the Wasteland in darkness, slowly, to shield our candles. I think of Tarkovsky's *Nostalghia,* how the man in a long dark coat tries two or three times to cross the empty natural pool with his flame intact. His feet slapping in the puddles, he protects the flame with his bare hand, sometimes with his coat, as if his life depends on it. When he finally succeeds, he plants the candle carefully on the edge of the pool and then collapses, his purpose served. If I reach the Wasteland with my flame intact, Candy will be there, a conviction that sustains me during the painstakingly slow march back home. I don't know what Rox is thinking.

22

THE FUNERAL HOME WON'T BUDGE until it hears from the official executor, never mind that Joseph has prepaid for cremation. What if Hoss returns to Toronto in an elevated state of bliss without checking voicemail? The only upside is it gives more time for Candy to discover my blog, read the veiled reference to Joseph's passing, and hit the road back to the Wasteland. Arriving, if the Gods are willing, before the funeral.

It almost sounds possible.

Rox drags me into an indoor flea market where she is drawn immediately to the vendor with vintage clothes. I flip through binders of black and white stills from the golden age of Hollywood, lingering over a classic image of Harold Lloyd dangling from the arms of a clock in *Safety Last!* Was he trying to hold on, or to stop time? Rox and I have managed to freeze-frame our lives, although the external world hasn't noticed. The store where she once replaced fallen scoops of ice cream has become a tattoo parlour. No second chances on offer there.

I SCAN FOR comments on my blog, for a hint Candy has understood. If I thought spraying my screen with lemon juice would help, I would do it. Candy wants to gain the upper hand by not announcing herself in advance. This would be the sister I know, always looking for an edge of control, the element of surprise.

Rox examines the labels of the *All My Children* tapes for an eventful episode, while I break out the Hungry Man Dinners. We have enough frozen food to hunker down here for a few weeks, if Candy is delayed. The goings-on at Pine Valley enthrall us for hours until we doze off on the couch. We're wrapped under the crocheted afghan, its web-like squares sticky with the honey-bourbon residue from my chicken strips and the spiced rum barbecue sauce from her popcorn chicken. I wake at four in the morning, alone. Family intrigue in Pine Valley continues, but feels empty without Rox's acerbic commentary.

Is Rox still here? The vibrations coming from Candy's room and that shake the paintings in the hall fill me with warmth. Rox is snoring on the cot, the empty bed overhead. It's comforting to know she has not barricaded the door. In my own bed, I grip both sides of the frame for safety, my head filled with images of Stuart Chandler's art gallery, Joseph and Mary in the field, my first lost brother Adam, me hanging from the minute hand of a clock.

IN THE MORNING Rox's cot is empty, but I dare not enter the room. I feel the same way standing at the entrance to my own bedroom in Montreal after Rox has left — a powerful sense that I do not belong here, so much so that I would grab clothes quickly from my dresser and closet, and leave the environment untouched.

Today I step across the threshold. A faint breeze wafts in through the open window competing with heat rays from the noonday sun, neither enough to mask Rox's country-girl scent. The sheets have been thrown back, partially draped over the bed above; the pillow holds the impression of her head; the knickknacks, jewellery, and old schoolwork on Candy's dresser are out of place, shifted by the night's vibrations. I manage to collapse onto Candy's bed. I sit there, my bare feet tucked under Rox's blanket. From this position, I see the edge of Candy's dresser and the floorboard that hides Phebe's time capsule.

Rox appears in the doorway with one towel wrapped around her body and another draped across her shoulders to catch the last drips from her hair. In the moment before she notices me, her body is uncharacteristically relaxed. She fairly floats into the room. Then our eyes meet, and her body tenses up so tightly the towel goes slack, and she has to pull it tightly around her. I am intruding into what has always been a private space for her and Candy; she is physically vulnerable. For the briefest of moments, I'm disappointed the figure is not Candy, although I'm pleased to see Rox still here, even if I blush at seeing so much of her skin.

My sister would not have worn a towel. Just as Hoss's

voice has never changed, Candy never lost her sense of childlike innocence about her body. I would often leave my bedroom only to stumble upon her nude in the hall. I came to dread these moments, and the inevitable flushing of my face. She seemed to take no notice of my presence, but for someone with such a keen sense of fashion, and an uncanny ability to draw people's gaze, she might have been conducting an experiment. At what precise moment would a nude body become naked? And when does a brother decide he shouldn't look? After all those sex scenes as Molly O, maybe Candy has grown self-conscious about her naked body. Prudish, even. Or I have. She needs to be held in medium shot, wrapped in shadow and framed obliquely before she is comfortable without clothes.

Rox drops her eyes to the floor and turns her head, wishing no doubt to disappear into the cubby hole with Phebe's daguerreotype. I look the other way, and angle out of the room without a word. In *As You Desire Me*, a stranger convinces Greta Garbo she's been suffering from amnesia. No one is sure of the truth. I could write a dictionary for all the words Rox and I don't say.

Our brunch is almost festive; Rox breaks out an open box of Aunt Jemima. As she flicks water in the pan to test it, I quietly check my blog again, pretending to protect the screen against the splatter rather than from Rox's gaze.

All through my early home life, Rox and Candy never sat down for breakfast; they preferred to slip out the door with an apple or a banana. Now Rox and I face off at the table with a plateful of pancakes.

— I'm sorry about Joseph. I don't know if I've said.

— He liked to think we were long-lost relatives of Cary Grant. But you know that. You spoke to him. You wrote. You visited.

— He loved you.

— When people die in winter, they have to wait until the ground thaws before they bury them. At least they used to. In summer, it's the body they have to keep cold.

— You told Hoss about Joseph, right? He'll be here soon. Then you can get on with it. I'm sick of living in limbo.

— All it takes is a signature to put me in charge. I can pretend to be him.

— I should go. I'm restless.

— Joseph would want you here.

— Would have wanted. You've been saying that a lot. I worry.

— Hoss is into this group called Momentous Moments. They have eliminated the past and future tense from their lexicon. All now, all the time.

— Hoss loves you, too.

— We're strangers. Ever since ...

— You need to stick together. The two of you.

— The three of us.

Rox doesn't answer, unsure, perhaps, if I mean her or Candy. I'm not sure either.

We both press our pancakes firmly into deep pools of syrup on our plates, the silence broken only by the scrape of our forks against porcelain as we hit bottom.

Molly O
The seductive cinema of Mickey Nailand

| Home | Films | Suppositions | About Me |

Musing aloud on the Dynamic Duo
Posted by LJ

Bergman with Bibi Andersson and Liv Ullman. Fassbinder with Ingrid Caven and Hannah Schygulla. Godard with Anna Karina and Anne Wiazemsky. Truffaut with Nathalie Baye and Fanny Ardant. Allen with Diane Keaton and Mia Farrow.

But for Nailand, only Molly O.

Molly O appears in all of Nailand's fifteen films, and her presence grows more charismatic, more powerful, and more indispensable with each work. There is a palpable power struggle in place — not just between the two as characters in a scenario, but between the director and "his" actress. Through sheer force of intelligence, wit, and sensuality, Molly O gives the films their edge — their very essence. She may well be the creative genius, not Nailand.

His first film, *Dyn Amic*, is less homage to Stephen Dwoskin's *Dyn Amo* than a fawning tribute — it is painfully clear Nailand has nothing new to offer about the voyeuristic power struggle between stripper and patron. Even the presence of Molly O can't save his debut from being derivative. Nailand might have ended his career right there, before it began, but he breaks new ground by adapting and reinventing the films of Mary Pickford.

As a co-founder of United Artists, Pickford was the most powerful woman of early Hollywood, and yet she still played traditional roles. Surely it is Molly O — not Mickey Nailand — who wants to pay homage to this pioneer of the silent screen, to comment on the gender and cinematic conventions that held Pickford in place, and to adopt a cinema of the erotic that was both breathless and Brechtian.

Given the banality of his upbringing in Shepardsville, I wonder if Mickey Nailand could have developed such an original cinematic language without a muse. Was she or wasn't she? Only Molly O knows for sure.

Leave a comment

23

WE SIT IN THE WICKER rocking chairs on the front step, Rox sketching gypsies from memory, me keeping my eyes peeled. An old habit. All those years, sitting on the porch after school before entering the empty house. Not wanting to face the void. Convinced if I stare long and hard enough Mary will reappear around the bend. And then Candy.

JOSEPH DID NOT permit us to watch Mary's cremation, so I invented my own versions. Sometimes local authorities burst in to arrest the funeral director. No, he protests, it was Joseph Grant, the grieving widower, who supplied the used coffin. It went unsold at his auction house last week. I imagine the chauffeur in *Burnt Offerings*, who grins so malevolently at the child during his mother's funeral, and I start to sweat and shake.

I WAKE WITH a shiver, neither the sun nor Rox in sight. Her

scent lingers. She can't have gone far. Small comfort. Her absence reminds me Joseph is gone permanently. I imagine him, waiting impatiently in the mortuary, wondering why it's taking so long for his final ride into the sunset. I'll give Hoss another day to finish his retreat, check his messages. Candy I give three. All his children.

I find Rox in the garage running her finger along the plastic tarp that covers the Steenbeck.

— I should go.

— You remember the film the two of you did?

— The three of us.

— Hoss will be here soon. We'll get things straightened out by sundown.

— That's a line from a vampire movie.

— *Star Trek TNG*. Hoss could tell you the Stardate.

— You're always quoting. Why don't you speak for yourself?

— I like what other people say better.

— Been here too long.

— You have a better place to be?

— Going, going, gone.

All I want is to pick up Chinese, watch another eight hours of *All My Children* with her, drop plum sauce on the afghan.

Rox snaps up the knapsack at her feet.

— You'll be back for the ceremony?

— Expect me when you see me.

— You're the one quoting now. I just can't quite remember what.

The image is so beautiful — passing from an abandoned editing machine in a somber barn into the fading light of a summer afternoon — that I simply watch her walk out of the frame. Then, in the baroque manner of a Eugène Green film, I remain still to record the vibration of her absence.

CANDY'S DOOR IS ajar. All is quiet and still. I pull up the baseboard, reach into the past to retrieve Phebe's message to the future. It's gone.

24

WILL CANDY TALK? I MEAN, with a voice. I believe so. After travelling all this way — frame by frame, mile after mile — she will be ready to tell us what happened. What was the catalyst? Why did she keep silent for so long?

Upon her arrival, my hands will be shaking, my eyes watering. Pathetically transparent. On rainy days, when we played *Old Maid*, I would hold the offending card a little higher than the others in my hand, thinking I could fool Candy into picking it. Her poker face had a thousand shades, depending on the character she adopted. Even Molly O herself is a creation. It's pointless to imagine who, and how, she will be, but I do anyway.

Her voice will be tentative at first, both from the physical act of talking and the emotional strength required to share her story. There will be hesitations and pauses; she will circle back and jump ahead. She'll wink in my direction. Anyone so immersed in deconstructionist erotic cinema would not tell a story front to back. A beginning, middle, and end, but not necessarily in that order. She may hide behind euphemisms, avoid our glances, laugh nervously. We must let her shape her own narrative, free of Mickey Nailand's obsessive demands, of any need to reveal anything she wants to keep private. Small lies might creep in. Lies she has told herself. In voicing them, she may stop, do a double-take, question the truth of her own experience. All is permitted. If her words fail, I have images. There could be details of the film productions she's forgotten. I will nudge her memory, gently. Who am I kidding? Candy could conduct a master class in the cinema of Mickey Nailand. She doesn't need a two-bit scholar to warm up the crowd with a pretentious introduction.

Upstairs, her wardrobe of vintage dresses is all dry-cleaned. There's a bottle of *Candy* eau de parfum on the nightstand — the special collector bottle with the hot pink wrist band that says "Give me Candy." Cheap marketing ploys are not beneath me.

She will need time to recover from the news of Joseph's passing and acclimatize to us again. We will not spread his ashes in the field right away. She may hold a grudge at how I manipulated her to return or resent I didn't mess with her head sooner. There is no accounting for every possible reaction. All I can do is set the stage as much as possible. Candy may be skittish, ready to bolt at the first sign of trouble. A flash of anger on my face. A look of indifference in Hoss. That's all it could take for her to dart off again. What's important is for the three of us to be blank slates. We don't want to frighten her off, not after all this time. Not again.

I won't be surprised if she's become an expert in feng shui and can tell us which direction to face before we spread the ashes. It would certainly mend some fences with Hoss if she has a spiritual bent. She may also be a traditionalist. Let her bring a member of the clergy to say the words that fail her.

25

I WAS BENT OVER THE Steenbeck, speeding up and slowing down until the motor kicked in properly and the film stopped stuttering. Behind me, Hoss leaned over Flicker, counting to three before releasing the spring-loaded plunger — long enough for his tingling fingers to pass on an extra lucky electrical charge to keep the ball in play, but not long enough to get burned. The Steenbeck grunted and ground where it should have run smoothly, while Flicker's bells and whistles — such an integral part of the pinball experience — no longer rang. Hoss provided his own bevy of sound effects, yelping, cursing, cajoling, and hooting.

As my machine settled down and the film stock followed its predictable journey through pulleys and rollers, Hoss watched his ball shoot off rubber bands and buzzers on its mad free-for-all across the faces of early Hollywood stars like Laurel and Hardy, W.C. Fields, and Edward G. Robinson. Ignoring the manufacturer's instructions, Hoss tilted Flicker to gain a few seconds of precious leverage and guided the ball towards the double bonus score.

Hoss prided himself on his rebellious nature, scoffed at my milquetoast attempts to curry favour with Candy. Whereas I accepted the universe was unfolding in the only way possible, he fought fate every inch of the way with his superstitious plunger rituals, illegal tilts, and last-ditch flipper action. Except that Flicker never kept proper score. The numbers stuttered backwards and forwards at will. No matter how many times Hoss made the lights flash or released captive balls, he could only track his success by how long the ball was in play. This heightened the stakes, as if he alone were judge and jury. He set up a clock on the wall, agonized when he didn't match his previous best time. I never looked at his clock, so immersed was I in the intricacies of editing on the Steenbeck. Time has no meaning for me.

STRANGE THAT I should end up intensely devoted to the past and the future. Hoss is now the ostensibly easy-flowing, non-judgmental one, trying hard to live in the moment and make everyone conform to his Candy-less view of the world.

IT WAS OUR first Christmas at the Wasteland with Joseph since Candy had disappeared seven years before. I was in graduate school writing a thesis on *Back to God's Country*, and Hoss was preaching a "Living Lightly on the Earth" regime, which he'd picked up from his first guru in Scotland.

While I was researching a classic slice of Canadian silent film history, Hoss was exhorting Joseph to jettison the Steenbeck as a way to expunge the past.

I suggested Hoss could start his expunging with Flicker and the four milk crates of records in our old bedroom. He had no comeback because he could not reveal his true agenda: to rid the Wasteland of any last remnants of Candy. But why? His resentment of Candy remained unaltered. Or maybe some part of Hoss was actually sad, and he turned his sadness into anger so he didn't feel the pain.

Joseph wouldn't throw anything out that might one day be useful or valuable. I suspected he also wanted to preserve the Wasteland as it was to help forget how many years had passed since Candy left. At least, that's how I would have felt in his shoes. For the same reason he never cleaned out her bedroom. On New Year's Eve, Hoss got high with old stoner friends rather than suffer through "Auld Lang Syne" with me and Joseph.

AFTER A TOUGH breakup in his thirties, Hoss came to Montreal so I could witness a ritual burning of photographs and letters from his ex. I was immersed in archival research for my doctorate on the personal cinema of Stephen Dwoskin. Destroying the past was the last thing I wanted to do, but my heated resistance only upped the stakes for Hoss. He sniffed out two shoeboxes of postcards and notes from my closet, and insisted I toss them into the fire. I called him a neo-fascist and he cut short his visit.

IN MY FORTIES, Hoss dragged me to one of his breathwork evenings in Toronto, ostensibly to rectify my shallow breathing, but really to dislodge Candy from my diaphragm, as if she were a stubborn fur ball. We were six men, sitting cross-legged in a circle, rocking to the sound of bad New Age music that slowly built to a climax. The short, deep breaths were supposed to lead to some natural high, a spiritual release, maybe an insight. My mind drifted to how Candy might have dressed as Jean Seberg in *Breathless*. Hoss hyperventilated, and ended in a coughing fit. I thought what he needed was more weed, not this breath shit. I waited at the door while Hoss and the other men hugged and then hugged some more.

HIS NEW LOVE interest, Tasha, got him to try channelling universal life force through his hands, something he only ever did before with a television remote. I was roped into being the guinea pig for their reiki workshop. The four of them had their hands all around me, and were so utterly serious that I started to think they could actually tell me something interesting. An old hippie with a pony-tail could see my aura, but was blind to the shimmering presence of Candy whom I'm certain was behind my shoulder; the redhead in her twenties heard voices, a completely useless talent to detect my silent sister; Tasha, whose long hair tickled my nose, had an innate sense of "knowing" but brought no news of Candy from beyond the beyond. And then there was Hoss, the dumbass Sergeant Shultz on *Hogan's Heroes*. He saw nothing. He heard nothing. He knew nothing.

In pursuit of Lindsay, he embraced Eye Movement Desensitization and Reprocessing. I suspected he took a shammy to his heart, wiping out all traces of his anger and hurt about Candy. He tried to get me interested, but I did not want to be desensitized or reprocessed. On the contrary, I was looking for more ways to bring Candy to the surface, and this "openness to possibility" was the very reason I discovered Molly O.

ALL THIS TIME I've been expecting Hoss to react to my presentation of Molly O with mild scepticism. He might actually be hostile. The sister who disappeared is back to steal the show once again. But an angry response might be a good thing: it would demonstrate that Hoss believes I've found Candy. And that would quell any of my own doubts that might bubble to the surface.

26

I INCH FORWARD, CHIN DRAGGING against the ground, head brushing against cobwebs and the underside of the boards, fingers clutching at dry earth. The crawlspace under the stage is still the coolest place on the property in summer, especially when I strip down to my underwear. I can't move my head, so I'm stuck staring out through the knothole into the empty space. What I'm doing here I'm not sure. I'm uncomfortable, claustrophobic, and dirty, and feeling stupid. There is so much of Candy in Molly O I can fairly say my sister will be too dignified to come back in here. If the crawlspace makes it onto her short list of childhood haunts to visit, she will simply cast a glance through the cracks or gently caress the boards.

No screeching brakes or blasting horn to mark its arrival, just a softly purring, eco-friendly coast into the front yard to nestle up behind my own rental. A discreet entrance as befits my silent sister. A door closes, followed by the slamming of the trunk, and then another passenger door shuts firmly. Candy has brought so much stuff it has overflowed from the trunk to the back seat — clothes, mementoes, gifts for all of us. She has come back to stay.

She's taking advantage of Joseph's absence to inspect her old home. The living room sofa, the new flat-screen television, the beanbag chair, the crocheted afghan, the Formica table, the kitchen chairs with the stuffing pushing through the cracked vinyl, the chalkboard with her prescient words — nothing escapes her scrutiny. It strikes her how so little has changed, how Joseph has been living in suspended time. She has an inkling of how her unexplained departure and prolonged absence have drained the life out of her family. No regrets for her choices, no remorse that we have paid so dearly for her freedom. She is overcome by the loss of never knowing her mother, the magnitude of her decision to leave all those long years ago. Yet I doubt she breaks down in tears at the threshold of the house.

By now she's spotting the cremation file on the kitchen table, and — ever the sensitive artist — is taking in the presence of death. No, it can't be! Joseph is simply planning ahead to take the burden off his children. She calls out to him with a plaintive cry. She stands in silence. If he's ill, the shock of hearing her voice at long last might push him over the edge. She heads up the stairs to disprove her worst fears, each step heavier than the last. More confusion: the master bedroom in disarray, her brothers' bedroom showing signs of occupancy and her own room apparently awaiting her arrival. No time now to make sense of it all. Without thinking, she slips on the pink "Give me Candy" bracelet.

The screen of the back door creaks open and slams shut. Her feet run towards the barn and the blur of her blue jeans crosses my line of vision. The knothole gives me a knee-high view, and she is not wearing Flapper-like rouge today. My first sighting is oh so brief!

— Joseph! LJ!

Candy's voice sounds remarkably like Hoss's high-pitched squeak.

— Where are they?

A woman's voice, hoarse, painful to take in. The first voice must in fact be Hoss, the second Candy. It explains so much. Out of shame for a voice damaged at birth Candy has embraced silence.

— They must have gone for a walk.

— Maybe something happened.

This is not Candy, only a new conquest from the island retreat. I'm equal parts disappointed and relieved to have my hopes dashed again. Perhaps the interloper will explore the field, lose her bearings, run in circles. Collapsing on the earth she will lie parched by day and dewy by night. We will dump her body into the quicksand later, after the wind dies.

— This is where you fell, right? Where it all started?

This is Hoss all over, sharing family intimacies with imperfect strangers. What stories about Candy has he carelessly revealed? A flash of white T-shirt and a yelp as he slips on a board and lands pretty much on the spot where he fell all those years ago. The past is never far behind. The woman bends over him, kneeling at knothole level, and the tattoo of a bird — maybe a cardinal — comes into view above her sacrum. Her sandy hair is gathered loosely in two bunches under a straw hat, making her look like a nine-year-old on her way to the waterhole. As she turns, her face is almost mime-white. I can't see her eyes. With powerful arms, she hauls Hoss off the ground. She is not one to wallow helplessly in quicksand.

Hoss places his hands a few inches from his back in some kind of energy-healing manoeuvre.

— Where the fuck are they?

My bare toes don't work the same way as my fingers. I wiggle left and right, and back and forth, but this only jams my body in tighter.

— Did you hear something?

Hoss bends with some difficulty to look through the knothole. I can't tell if he's happy to see me. Having been desensitized and reprocessed, his eye movement is difficult to read.

— Anthea, meet Little Joe, my little brother who seems to be having a little trouble.

Her pupil is dilated. Fatigue or pharmaceuticals?

— Janardan told me to expect anything and everything at the Wasteland.

— Jann Arden told you that?

— Janardan is Sanskrit for "one who helps people." Your brother just got anointed this weekend by our leader, Ashok.

— A shock for me, too. I prefer Janardan's given nickname.

— Sorry?

— Don't listen to LJ. He's not himself.

— That makes two of us. Maybe three.

She doesn't know he's gone by Hoss all his life, and doesn't get the *M*A*S*H* reference. I give their relationship until the fall TV season.

— If you're such a helper, get me out of here.

— We might need the jaws of life.

Anthea's voice is solemn. Possibly mocking. The jaws of life won't help Joseph. Why hasn't Hoss asked about our father? Why has he brought a date two days after his death? My voicemail was clear. Something about the need to come home urgently. Did I have to spell it out? He understands too well. Knowing Joseph is dead means there is no need to rush home. No need to inquire after his health. Every reason to bring a love interest for moral support because he does not want to be alone with me and the ghosts.

— I'll find something in the barn. Keep an eye on LJ.

I can see myself reflected in Anthea's right pupil — a film professor trapped in the earth under the auction stage peeping out a knothole, desperate to connect with the spores of his childhood.

— We came as fast as we could when we got your message. I don't normally sound so raw. I lost my voice with all the screaming at the retreat. Do you mind if we just wait quietly? Or you can talk, if you want. Tell me his other nickname.

My identity-rich brother returns a few moments later with an axe.

— Stand back.

His squeaky voice lacks all authority, and Anthea doesn't budge.

— Maybe you should aim away from LJ.

— Do you want to do it then?

The vibration from Anthea's first blow pushes my head higher against the boards. It takes another four swings to break through the wood. I scramble out into the fading afternoon light, the two of them towering above me. Awaiting explanations, no doubt. I stand there, bare chest and legs dusty with dry earth, knees wobbly from lack of circulation.

— Don't tell me Joseph is down there with you.

— Joseph is dead.

27

HOSS'S STORYLINE FOR OUR FAMILY is unwavering, fixed for all time with the word "disappeared" carrying its own beginning, middle, and end. In a hundred workshops and retreats, he has processed, shared, and resolved. Sufficiently recovered from his own trauma, he helps others, using the unique healing qualities he has managed to harness in his hands. He will deftly brush off any turn in the conversation that's heading towards Candy as Kwai-Chang Caine wards off blows in *Kung Fu*. If not, if unsuccessful, the protective bubble so painstakingly constructed through endless therapies, gurus, and guides might burst, and painful feelings about Candy will leach out.

So now is not the time to talk about Candy, although in my dreams his shock over Joseph's passing will incite him to speak about her, and I will be able to give him the happy news. Hoss has seen every episode of *L.A. Law* and, despite any nuances between the American and Canadian legal systems, or any differences between television and reality, he will dismiss all my evidence about the Candy-Molly O connection as circumstantial. Not because he disbelieves, but rather because he does not want to believe. To accept Candy as Molly O, and to embrace her return to the fold, will demand more than Hoss can manage. We will have words. If Candy does not arrive in a timely fashion, he will push forward with Joseph's funeral, whatever my own wishes.

He will cross-examine me, and I have made a thorough list to counter every possible objection. Yes, Nailand might have shown up at the auctions to witness Candy's silent performances, and then stolen her essence for his films. It's possible he found an actress who resembled Candy and taught her to walk backwards and wear white gloves. Or perhaps Porky really is a Lester Young aficionado, hoping to come across some original recordings of Prez on Aladdin or Savoy at our auctions, and Mickey Nailand never set foot near the Wasteland.

But then who came up with all the names? The girl squatter in *Tess of the Storm County* is Rox, the man in *Daddy Long Legs* is Joseph, the amorous nephew in *Oh, Uncle* is Lewis. One name might have been a coincidence, but all three?

And what about Candy's fascination for Tin Pan Alley, how she starts playing "The Bad in Every Man" over and over, the tinny sound passing easily through our shared wall? That song is a draft for the more celebrated "Blue Moon," a few bars of which appear towards the end of Nailand's *Little Princess*. I wonder if Nailand and Candy plant all these clues to amuse themselves or to lay breadcrumbs for me. I have played the album backwards at different speeds, ears tuned for clues among the jumbled sounds. If the Beatles could plant secret messages, why not Rodgers and Hart? What will seal the deal for Hoss, however, are the snippets of King Crimson and the homage to our family theme song in *Little Red Riding Hood*.

I know the where, the when, the what, and the who. All I'm missing is the why.

Molly O
The seductive cinema of Mickey Nailand

| Home | Films | Suppositions | About Me |

Love and Theft
Posted by LJ

Oh yes, the music. Very strange, completely out of keeping
with a silent film and thus designed to distance the viewer
and undermine the erotic. More than that, the music often
amplifies the conflict between the two main characters
and the actors, Nailand and Molly O. It typically evokes
theft, reinforcing the question of ownership. Molly O can
never be bought, traded, or sold. She is too powerful. She is
inseparable from the films. Without her, they do not exist.

For *Little Red Riding Hood* and *One Hundred Percent American*,
Nailand steals songs that have already been stolen. In the
former, he uses fragments of King Crimson's "Larks' Tongues
in Aspic, Part Two," previously appearing illegally in the
erotic film *Emmanuelle*. Of course, by cutting in and out of the
piece, Nailand uses it ironically — a far cry from *Emmanuelle*'s
attempt to convey sexual build-up through the music. Since
her riding hood appears in black and white, Nailand also

throws in the opening chords from Crimson's "Red" for a blast of colour. Little Red Riding Hood hesitates in the forest, studies a map, and then confidently burns it, all this to the strains of the celebrated theme song of *Bonanza*; she lights her match at the moment in the score when Hoss, Little Joe and the others burst through the burning parchment on their horses in the show's opening credits. In *One Hundred Percent American*, to echo the "coming and going" of the auction and the sex, he inserts excerpts from the breathy "Je t'aime … moi non plus" by Serge Gainsbourg, who himself stole liberally from classical music. In *Little Princess*, Nailand throws in a few bars of "Blue Moon," a song in which Rodgers and Hart steal from their own earlier composition. All these references to theft give one pause about the real-life relationship between Nailand and Molly O: who or what has been stolen, by whom, and for what greater purpose?

Leave a comment

28

WHAT IS CANDY'S GREATER PURPOSE? If she wants to hide from us forever, then why plant these clues? They can only mean she wants to be found. Maybe she's like one of those old Russian Cold War sleepers who waits decades for a sign from the Mother Country to carry out a long-planned assault on democracy. Except in her case, the signal awakens dormant memories and desires. My blog is that homing device; it will find her. Love may or may not have been good to her. After such an intense and claustrophobic experience with Nailand, she may well have opted for a peripatetic life, passing through a series of lovers in Denver, Portland. Other places. I give her a week to cross the International Date Line. She will make a grand entrance, or she won't. I'm sure she will. Her presence will bring my brother down a notch. To see his self-assured face blanch, to hear his squeaky voice rise to a fever pitch and his hands heat up, to witness him stand there, quivering.

HOSS SITS ON the top tier staring mournfully at the Wasteland, oblivious to the sorry spectacle unfolding behind his sore back. Anthea walks deliberately, one foot in front of the other, a pirate measuring out paces to buried treasure. When she reaches the edge of the stage, she does an about-face, and crosses back again. In the guise of giving my brother space to deal with the bad news, she is doing her best to take up every inch of the territory that's left to her. Anthea's military gait, so foreign to the spirit whose feet once graced these boards, makes me want to stick out my foot and watch the resulting tumble off the edge. X marks the spot. Nursing her bruised sacrum, she could then truly understand how it all got started.

HOSS SLIPS INTO the house alone. Anthea stops parading and starts with questions, which I answer with the clipped efficiency of a policeman forced to speak with crime reporters. No context, no tawdry anecdotes, nothing to allow entry into the inner Grant sanctum. She has the decency to blush, and the heat melts a layer of sunscreen from her cheeks.

— We're not supposed to have relations at retreats. It disturbs the energy. But I had a kink in L5, and Janardan has these amazing hands. They're like hot stones that move. Normally I would have a roommate, but there were only nine of us on the island. One for each number of the Enneagram. The place was so big it had separate floors for women and men. No one knew. We were quiet. But Janardan decides to fess up in the morning sharing circle. He apologized to Ashok and the whole group for his lack of self control.

He couldn't look Ashok in the eye. Especially after he got recognized the day before for all he'd done for Momentous Moments. Ashok's sound system is finicky. Janardan is the only one who can make it work. We call him the Keeper of the Music. Totally helpful. He's such a Two. Has he always been like that? We could all see there were father-son issues going on, big time. Everyone except Janardan. The apple doesn't fall far from the septic tank. Ashok was totally cool with the transgression. But then he really pushed home that living in the moment means seizing the moment and then Janardan has this sudden panic that he will be too late to see your father. Your message freaked him out. I told him to call you, to find out what's so urgent. He just cranked the music and floored it. I don't know speeds in metric, but it was scary fast. I felt like I was talking to a wall. Completely zoned out. Like a deep meditation except he could have run someone over. I had never seen him like that. Have you? He wanted me to come to meet your father. Now I don't know why I'm here. I'm walking on eggplants.

— Eggshells.

Piercing guitar chords wrapped in the thick mist of the English moors issue forth from the open bedroom window.

— Maybe it's a call for help. Should I go see him?

— It's Jethro Tull *Thick as a Brick*, side two. I would not disturb him.

Where does Hoss find these women? How could he bring a date to Joseph's funeral? All right, my message was vague. Still. He must have expected Joseph to be in a weakened state, still unable to talk and with no interest in exchanging notes with his new girlfriend. Not unless she has some voodoo medicine to restore Joseph's voice and repel the remaining invaders from his throat once and for all.

I don't see Anthea offering much of anything. So far she has mutilated the crawl space where Candy and I used to lie in the cool earth and she's trampled on the last traces of Candy's performances. I won't give her any credit for rescuing me since I could have backed out on my own, given time.

Hoss cranks up the speakers. I know what's coming. The climax, where the busy musical arrangements suddenly stop and Ian Anderson sings *a cappella* in a dramatic offer to help pick up our dead. This is Hoss all over. Indulging in a progressive rock rendition of death, instead of being here in the flesh to help me ride Joseph out of the field. But when the record ends, and silence ensues, I leave Anthea on the stage all the same. Maybe it is a call for help after all.

The sock drawer is askew. A plaid lumberjack shirt has been removed from the closet. The mirror is off the wall, revealing an empty cubbyhole. Judging from the *Playboys* strewn on the bed, he's even taken up the loose board where we hid our stash from the curious eyes of Candy and the judgmental frowns of Joseph. All of the room's hiding places, in other words, have been thoroughly ransacked. Not true. Hoss is on his knees prying up the baseboard, inspecting a space that even I didn't know about. It's never too late to learn something about a sibling. I sense this is not the right moment, and walk backwards out of the room, silently, in my best imitation of our sister.

THE THREAT OF skin cancer diminished, Anthea has changed into full-length clothes to ward off mosquitoes spreading the West Nile and Zika viruses. So far, she has not been bitten, although she could hear them around her head throughout the guided meditations on the island. She wasn't supposed to swat them, only focus on her fear.

Her tie-dye shirt, two sizes too big, has a mash-up of psychedelic swirls that would repel any sentient being. This loose upper-body garment is at odds with the form-fitting purple leggings, which show off her chiselled limbs and draw attention to how short they are. The kind of outfit Candy would not be caught dead in.

Anthea makes a salad from the remnants of pale green Iceberg lettuce and pink hothouse tomatoes in the refrigerator, waving off the Hungry Man options. I make a mental note to stock up on fresh frozen food for Candy.

Hoss is reverting to a primitive state, the kind of insular and numb being he has worked so hard to leave behind. He stares at his Buffalo chicken strips, fork hanging limply between his fingers. All that's missing are the headphones.

— Just be with whatever is happening for you, as Ashok says.

Knowing Hoss, he is clicking through all the scenes of paternal deaths from the vast archive of television shows in his head. He falls into the category of all the sons who arrive too late to the deathbed. Except he didn't know Joseph was dying so there is guilt at having spent three days at the retreat. He may catch glimpses of Joseph out of the corner of his eye, and think of the ghostly afterimages on television when channels start to break down, and characters from one show seemingly cross into another. But that's me guessing. I don't really know.

— I lost my father when I was twenty. It's a terrible blow. You feel you're never going to get over it. But then you do. Time —

— What's with the you, you, you? Own your own fucking experience, it's nothing to do with mine.

He chases the chicken strips around the plastic compartment like a Sioux warrior forcing a buffalo over a cliff to its death. When the pieces do leap over the barrier to crash into the mashed potatoes, Hoss spears them with his fork to make sure they're dead.

— If you hadn't made me stop for sunscreen, I might have got here in time.

Anthea inhales sharply a few times, unable to get a full breath. She finds her purse in the living room and takes a few shots from her puffer, then disappears upstairs.

— Nice going, Jann Arden.

Hoss jumps up, pivots, and takes four strides towards the back door before turning to deliver his retort.

— You can't smell *E. coli*. You can't see it or taste it. Sometimes you don't even know you're infected until it's too late and your kidneys start to shut down. When was the last time you had the water tested? I'm going to order an autopsy.

He spots the blackboard, with "Rx. Later" carefully preserved.

— This is the real poison. Never letting go. You're filled with the same shit. So here's how I'm going to help you. We're going to cremate Joseph and get rid of this place, and everything in it. Then we can all start living in the moment.

I don't need your help, you philistine. Candy is alive, and will be here momentarily.

29

THE AUGUST 1979 DOROTHY STRATTEN issue was the pride of our collection. We were enamoured of her nude poses long before she was named Playmate of the Year, and I liked to think that Hugh Hefner himself made the final selection. He left the hot tub in the Playboy Mansion, slipped on a robe, and, lighting his pipe, said, "Yes, she's the one, the girl from Vancouver." I took out the magazine whenever Hoss went on a bender, and Rox was in seclusion with Candy. Although Rox's voice through the walls could shake my hands, and I had to take care not to tear the pages.

It was the first time someone we felt we knew intimately had been murdered. I look at the photos, so still now. Innocent family snapshots, the list of turnoffs that includes jealous people. Dorothy never saw it coming. Naive girl, and slimy impresario turned ex-husband. Do I hear an echo in the relationship between Candy and Mickey Nailand? No, I like to think they were good together. It's what happens after he dies that I can't fathom.

— I HAD A teacher who talked through laryngitis and wrecked his voice. I don't want a permanent rasp like him. My voice is getting better, don't you think?

Anthea scans her iPod for eco music, either rainfall or crashing waves. Then she dives into a book on breathwork, turning each page with a forceful exhale. She keeps up a steady rhythm until a moth flits inside the lampshade.

— Your screens are okay, right? I didn't want to spend the extra money for health coverage. If I have problems here, I am royally fucked. I'm having a prolonged healing crisis. Chicken pox last year. Now I've hurt my tonsils. If they come out, it's ice cream for a week and I put on five pounds. My wisdom teeth are next. At the retreat, I felt a twinge on the right side of my mouth. Did Janardan say when he'll be back?

More than ever, I miss Candy's silence, the way she lets gestures and movement speak for her. All those Sunday afternoons together on the couch watching classic films on PBS, the hint of a smile during the screwball comedies, the feigned yawn to hide the tear during the three-hanky melodramas, the urgent notes on what the actresses were wearing.

The patrons all saw the stylized "G" on Candy's frilly black tutu as an echo of the giant letter perched above the archway to Grant's Auction Service rather than as a nod to Louise Brooks in *Now We're in the Air*. The night Candy sat on an oak barrel in a satin dress and top hat, raising a knee to reveal a garter belt, no one shouted out "Falling in Love Again." Nor did anyone tell her to "put the blame on Mame" during her glove striptease.

None of it mattered to Candy who, as a true artist, delivered performances primarily for herself, and then for Rox and me. Probably she took secret pleasure in mystifying the riff raff. Brooks's false innocence, Dietrich's calculated androgyny, Hayworth's tamed spontaneity — Candy captured it with a few telling motions.

— Janardan told me you show movies in college.

— I teach film in university.

— I do waste outreach in Buffalo.

She grabs a cushion and sets up on the floor cross-legged.

— I should have gone straight to the floor. I was trying to be polite. Take me as I am. Isn't that what Joni Mitchell says?

Candy's posture has always been perfect. She would bring silverware to her mouth — not like the rest of us who would bend our heads to the table. Whereas I would wait for the bathroom slumped against the wall, she would stand dead centre in the hall, unencumbered and free. Still Life with and without Towel.

— Sometimes I get fed up with the yoga postures, the breathing, the meditation, all this living in the fucking moment. I met your brother at a silent retreat two years ago. Not even. I saw his eyes through a burka. A few dates, a few treatments with those magic hands and I'm ready to apply for refugee status in Toronto. I am so not grounded. Just when I was getting used to being a Four, Ashok says I'm a Six. Sixes are afraid, Fours are depressed. I'd say you're a Five. A seeker of knowledge, a little detached.

It must have taken tremendous strength of will to be Candy. Not just for the vow of silence, but also for the stamina required to get through each day. She would never drop out of character — whether surrounded by thousands of hostile eyes at school or crossing our front yard with me watching from behind the boulder. Without access to a character's voice, her performances are anchored in wardrobe and body language. I see it all before me. It draws me in. How I anticipate her costume changes. Then, amid the awe and admiration, I experience a sliver of disappointment barely sufficient to register. It takes a while, decades, to understand I'm wanting Candy to wear my mother's clothes again. That was the original costume, and the best.

— We're supposed to have all the numbers within us so it's no big deal. I'm only disappointed Ashok didn't get it right the first time. I feel jerked around. You get invested in a certain idea of yourself and then, poof, it's yanked away. Knowing Janardan has another name besides Eric really bothers me. I don't want to know what it is anymore.

— Hoss, after the big dumb brother on *Bonanza*. No one's ever called him Eric. I don't believe in the Enneagram. I'm a free man, not a number.

In my irritation, I've botched the reference to *The Prisoner*. I miss Hoss. He would never let that kind of mistake go unremarked.

— Everyone has a number. Some people want to see themselves as unique is all. They can't bear the idea that their lives are part of a larger pattern. Just saying.

— Who is Number One?

— Even Steven. That's one of the grounding principles of Momentous Moments. No judgment, no hierarchies. We are where we need to be. Do you think I should call Janardan on his cell or give him more space?

Candy has never needed a retreat to discover herself, find her path, or be in the moment. All of her borrowed identities — from the auction stage to Molly O's films with Mickey Nailand — have only served to fuel the creativity burning inside her. Her continual reinvention, distortion, and camouflage make her impossible to pin down. Far from hiding her essence, the perpetual movement has made and kept her truly alive. As an artist, she has always been her own best creation.

— I'm trying not to call my son. He's with his father this weekend upstate. They barely know each other. They both sing. Is music enough to bond over? He's sent money all these years. I give him that much.

Why am I so convinced that Candy's transition back into our family will be easy? I've sprayed myself with a new-and-improved product that wipes away all traces of doubt or my money back. Now the damned spots on my collar won't come out, mosquitoes are lighting on my arm, and grey hairs are being unmasked despite all my attempts to stop time. Is she or isn't she coming? Only Candy knows for sure.

— I am truly sorry about your father. And your sister, too. We did some family sculpting this weekend, and Janardan chose me to play Candy. I was so honoured. It was a real gift. I would have been happy just to hold space for him so he could work through his stuff. But Ashok gave me a signal to break Candy's silence. He is so intuitive. He knows exactly when to push us to find an inner truth. So I trusted myself. I said, "I love you." Janardan broke down. It was beautiful. He had been holding on to Candy without knowing. Now he has totally let her go. I felt so close to him. If only we hadn't stopped. It's my pigment. No one talks about the hole in the ozone anymore.

— Let me tell you exactly why you're here. You are a projection, nothing more, nothing less, the latest in a long line of women whom Hoss has chosen to represent our sister. Hoss wanted Joseph to see his daughter one more time, that's why he brought you. In his eyes, you are the perfect choice, putting the words in her mouth that he has longed to hear all his life. The good news is he's only pissed off at you because he's seeing Candy. Whether you use I-language or not, you — Anthea — do not exist.

The way Anthea gets up from the cushion wordlessly and retreats in silence is likely the closest she has come to embodying my sister's character.

CANDY TURNED HER head at the precise moment the clump of grade ten boys protecting me from view stepped from the hallway into an alcove of lockers. Exposed as the sibling stalker, I feigned indifference to her gaze of contempt and pretended our encounter was by chance. What I really wanted was a reaction, to hear her shout and scream at my intrusiveness. But no. She accepted me as a hanger-on, perhaps secretly welcomed it. The warning bell rang, and

I needed to run to the other side of the school for my own class. I lingered instead, watching the girls take their places at the back of the row next to the window. Candy took the coveted last seat with Rox just ahead. While Rox opened her geometry set and slipped a pencil inside a compass, Candy stared at the parking lot. Had Mickey Nailand already made contact with her at this early date? At lunch break, they met in his Dodge Coronet to map out their future. Was she attracted to him for his soul, his body, for what he represents, or not at all? It's hard to believe Nailand had already formed his avant-garde approach to erotica. Chances are his ideas were still vague, especially given the derivative nature of his debut. His patter was smooth, hypnotic in its own way as her father's chant. It flattered her, this unadulterated male attention. Unlike Joseph, of course, Nailand directed his considerable charm at Candy herself rather than at nameless auction-goers. Nailand had been one of these patrons, watching Candy and her father exert their dual effect on the helpless crowd. Nailand promised Candy a bohemian life, where she could push her artistry so much further. Did she understand the nature of her future roles? Or had she already in mind a strategy to push Nailand in unimagined creative directions? He pressured her to leave. She would choose her moment of departure. No one else.

If I had spotted the two of them in his car, would I have intervened? Deprive Candy of her chance at stardom? Or would my blundering big brother act have pushed her away faster. I was never certain if my presence, or its absence, was in her best interests. I too walked on eggplants.

ANTHEA HAS LEFT her shoes at the bottom of the stairs rather than wear them into the bedroom. In her anger and hurt, she still observes social niceties. A gesture that makes me regret my outburst all the more. It can't be easy for her. She arrives at the childhood home of her new love interest only to find future father-in-law recently demised and brother-in-law-to-be trapped beneath a stage in his underwear. Her love interest has a name she doesn't know about — and names matter to her — then he falls into a mute trance and disappears in a huff. Instead of offering comfort and hospitality, little brother growls, snaps, and bites, declaring her a nonentity. Not even the water in the Wasteland can be trusted.

The delayed shame in my gut, the realization that I am a first-class heel, is too much to bear. I need to feel better. I head upstairs with a bottle of the good stuff to make amends with Anthea.

Explosive caramel on top, musky middle, and vanilla foundation — the triple effect they promised on the box. Having availed herself of Candy's perfume, Anthea is holding up one of my sister's vintage dresses against her own pint-sized body. With every motion, the pink "Give me Candy" bracelet slides up and down her wrist. Joseph kept an antique .22 in his closet. No safety catch. Loaded. I could tell police I thought Anthea was an intruder, which is, in fact, the truth.

— The door was open. It's not like she's going to wear this again.

— Candy never wears the same dress twice, at least not without changing an accessory. I'm surprised you don't know that; you, who presume to inhabit the skin of my sister. But your assumed knowledge is skin-deep, and not even the perfume that you've purloined can ...

With the economy of motion I've come to expect, Anthea rips the bracelet off her wrist and flings it, Frisbee style, at my face. Then she grabs my peace gesture from the tray, twists off the cap, and squirts Perrier behind her ears.

— Are you happy now? What a fucking house this is.

I can distinguish between the burst of anger on top, the mid notes of embarrassment, and the vanilla-inflected hurt at the base. But with her face all wet, it's hard to separate the fizzy water and *eau de parfum* from the salty tears.

Joseph's door squeaks before it slams shut. Let her sleep in the bed of a dead man while I repair the damage she has wrought. The pink bracelet has landed — significantly, I think — within a foot of the loose board that hid Phebe's time capsule. I rub off all traces of Anthea's fingerprints and replace the bracelet on the nightstand, next to the perfume, which I readjust so the label will be the first thing Candy sees. I brush down and hang back up the little black dress Anthea unceremoniously dropped to the floor. The sweet scent of Candy's perfume cannot penetrate my nostrils since they are stuffed. Tears roll down my face. What if this impersonation of my sister is as good as it gets or, worse, a harbinger? Abrasive, unequivocal, verbose, and vulgar. I could not bear it if Candy turned out this way. What about the inner contradictions, the dark mystery, the refined intellect? I want her home intact.

30

THE OPPRESSIVE HUMIDITY OF THIS summer night ends at the edge of the field. Once I pass through the rope barrier, and trek towards the flat rock, the temperature will drop. It will be pleasant at first, but then grow uncomfortably cool. I'll be shivering soon enough, my hands dry and chapped, especially if the wind picks up. Apart from the extra candles, flashlight, water, snacks, compass, and GPS, I've packed a fleece, windbreaker, and wool gloves. The rope around my waist won't help get me there, only guide me back. Wasn't it just the other day I was dragging out Joseph's body? I don't know where the time goes. Maybe it doesn't.

The first few minutes are the most dangerous because I'm tempted to look at the auction stage from behind. I will imagine Candy in one of her costumes, walking backwards towards me. I hold on to the image until the emptiness of the stage blots it out. But by that time, all my weight on one spot has stirred up manure buried in the soil from the time of Phebe, Lewis, and Isaac, and released methane. I won't see or smell it, but I know it's there. My legs go rubbery, my vision blurs, and the steady beat of my heart is replaced by syncopation worthy of vintage King Crimson. If I don't move quickly, I can get confused about what I'm doing out here.

The moon is on my side tonight; it reveals the rock to be a stone's throw away. This lifts all temptation to look back. I march smartly, testing the ground ahead with my walking stick. Without warning, the earth might simply open up into a dark chasm. I tap gently so as not to arouse ire. No one has ever been welcome here, except perhaps Joseph. Maybe we should have done something to drain out the poison. Sometimes it's better not to mess around. The Wasteland likes things as they are. I often think of *Frogs*, the film with Ray Milland as the bitter patriarch who refuses to accept that nature is rebelling. The others escape, leaving Milland in his wheelchair on his island to face the spiders, snakes, and other angry reptiles, alone and helpless. Joseph never disrespected the Wasteland, but it killed him anyway. Unless it didn't. Was the field always a danger zone or did the warnings only start after Mary died? How much easier was it to instill in his children a fear of the mystical qualities of the Wasteland than for Joseph — a busy widower — to keep an eye on them. My obsessive precautions may be as meaningful as Hoss's superstitious pinball tactics. But the Wasteland isn't the Flicker machine and I cannot deny the moment I step into the field I taste bile and my throat constricts. The moment I stop believing in the power of the Wasteland over life and death is the moment its power will be unleashed.

I can't see my feet now in the warm mists settling around my ankles. Around my head, where the air is thinner, it's getting colder. I'm more than halfway when a cloud comes out of nowhere, covering the moon and turning off the heat. I could see my breath if there were any light. Sinking to my knees comes naturally. It's warmer down here and I feel less exposed. This subservient position also suggests humility, which might be a good idea about now. Too awkward to crawl with a flashlight so I pull out my Blackberry as a talisman. It's slow going because it only reveals the few inches of ground directly in front and the light keeps going off, but it's got an old photo of Candy as the wallpaper.

I STUMBLE UPON the rock, my hands sliding across its smooth surface, just as my Blackberry dies. I had recharged it earlier in the day. My watch, too, has stopped. The flashlight batteries, which I tested, are also dead. The GPS says I'm in the middle of nowhere. From the other side of the fence, I hear a frog.

It takes me so long to strike a match I start to think the Wasteland doesn't like basic technologies either. But it's just that my fingers, raw from the crawling and numb from the cold, won't cooperate. I sit on the stone, holding the candle to keep warm. What was I thinking? That coming out here, under duress, would prove my worthiness to Candy? That, upon arriving home, instead of entering the house, she would inspect the auction stage and spot the light in the distance? That she would understand, intuitively, it was me out here, and follow the rope? That sitting on this cold forsaken rock in the dead of night would render our reunion all the more bittersweet? That everything has a price?

In my place, Hoss would probably start meditating. Focus on the breath. Don't fight the discomfort. Embrace the fear. Be in the moment. I would like to see how far all that New Age hokum would get him out here in the Wasteland. I don't imagine he ran out here when he stormed off. He probably drove to the Night Brew in Shep to score some pot for old times' sake and is now wandering around the empty parking lot like a character in a Jethro Tull song, vacantly scuffing his toes on packs of cigarette papers that fell out of trouser pockets long ago. The more he tries to forget Candy, the more he remembers. He has feelings to burn, which get filtered through the haze of his joints. Not only does the pot cool his hands, it softens the edges of his rage. Because surely that's what his ambivalence to Candy has always been about: how she stole the life of our mother, and then elevated herself to star of the household. Again, this unpleasant sensation in my gut that Hoss will not welcome Molly O into our midst.

HOSS AND I stood in the far end of the yard, on the edge of the Wasteland, both of us doubled over — me in a fit of coughing, him in a fit of laughter. He was fourteen and I was two years younger, though I never felt so close to him again. The feeling lasted five minutes, broken by Candy's appearance. All of ten years old, she was drawn by the tiny fire in the night sky and the sound of Hoss giggling without the laugh track of a prime-time sitcom, a first for her.

Hoss and I were transfixed under the light of the moon, embarrassed, guilty. It wasn't bad enough that he was indoctrinating his little brother to the wonders of weed, now there was little Candy about to reach for the roach clip. Just as she opened her mouth, as if to speak, Hoss moved towards her. I didn't know what he had in mind. She fled, straight into the field, and disappeared.

My giddiness from the half-inhaled joint went up in smoke. Paranoia set in, but I couldn't move my legs to chase after her. I looked to my older brother for steel-eyed resolve. He had all the get-up-and-go of an extra in a Cheech and Chong movie. Had this been his plan all along — to scare Candy into foolish choices?

I ran along the perimeter, calling out every few seconds. There was no hair shirt in sight so I let the rope burn the palm of my hand. Every so often I stopped and listened to the night. There was no swirling dust, no fog, or mist, but I could not penetrate the darkness or overcome my fear of plunging over the edge.

— We'd better get Joseph.

Hoss lowered his squeaky voice a few notches in a desperate bid to exude auctioneer-like confidence. I smelled his fear, and heard the second thoughts at his dastardly plan to resculpt our family. I ducked under the rope and threw myself into the void, falling flat on my face. The land was dry that night. I was still afraid of stumbling into a pit of quicksand. Hoss's voice became ever fainter as I moved deeper and deeper into the field. I refused to imagine the worst.

I am not sure how long it took to reach the stone or how I managed to find it. I only know she was waiting for me. She took my hand and squeezed it tight. I had proved myself to her. She sat, covered in dust and damp earth, placing her hands where we had spread Mary's ashes. I joined my hands with hers. She, too, missed our mother. For the first time I stepped out of my own lingering grief. At least Hoss and I had known Mary. We did not carry the guilt of causing her death. We sat a while. I heard Hoss calling for both of us. It felt good.

She led me back through the dark without a false step. It was the last time I felt so close to her, because soon after Rox would get top billing. That night ruptured something with Hoss. A week later he smoked up before the auction and fell off the stage, effectively starting Candy's acting career. I can't forgive him for that either.

IF I BURN myself, would she come home faster? I wave my finger through the flame, sit close for the faint warmth it projects. Hot wax drips evenly onto the rock and then flows into darkness. It follows the downward slope of the rock, rolling with the impenetrable force of lava into the dead soil.

I light another candle and, when it burns out, another. The wind is still, the ground sleeps. The thin air magnifies and distorts sound. When I throw my voice, "Candy!" bounces at me from all directions and at all volumes. So close I scooch over to make room for an unexpected visitor. So distant and faint, my heart aches. Here. I'm right here.

I'm trying to decide whether my last candle is half

burned or half intact when I hear a motorcycle. It must be on the concession road, but I can't get a fix on it. Either the Wasteland is playing tricks again or the bike is speeding up and slowing down over and over. It's avoiding rocks and craters, searching for its destination. Now both louder and slower and lacking the distinctive two-piston pop of a Harley, this is unquestionably a touring bike meant to carry long-lost sisters to their far-off childhood homes. Perhaps it has a sidecar for extra luggage. My paltry imagination has carved out no space for such a grand entrance.

My candle has drawn the bike past my car to the back of the stage, just as I'd hoped. The headlight is not strong enough to penetrate the barrier of the Wasteland. About three-quarters of the way to the rock it dissipates, but not before she has pulsed out the dots and dashes for "CQD" — the signal that came into use during the silent film era. *All stations: distress.* The perfect choice to announce her trepidatious return, but why has she waited so long to light the beacons? She switches off the headlight and tugs the rope. I tug back, hoping she ties it around her waist so I can reel her in. Seconds later, the rope is limp in my hands. She must be going it alone.

I imagine her motorcycle boots leaving an unforgiving imprint of their tread. But it's the swish of her nylon pants that signals her imminent arrival. Considering she is relying on long-term memory and instinct, she's taking hugely confident strides in the darkness. The Wasteland does not care for arrogance. Small craters, rocks, and hills appear without warning on the well-trod path, forcing the heartiest adventurer off stride and ever closer to the quicksand pits. She's forgotten. It makes me sick to think she might blow it all in the home stretch. I hold out the candle, with its failing light, as far as my arm can stretch.

What takes me hours of crawling on all fours Candy completes in minutes. My feeble candle picks up the orange reflective patches on her motorcycle vest. We have brought you back alive. A whiff of gas fumes from a hard day on the road wafts past me. The *eau de parfum* has turned into a better homecoming present than I could have imagined. Although she's left her helmet behind, her face is obscured by the poor light, as if the ghost of Mickey Nailand has followed along just to mess with my head one last time.

The boots have boosted her height. From what I can tell through the vest, time has left her flat chest intact. Surprising, as Molly O is more developed. The moon appears! Not a wrinkle, not a blemish. Time hasn't stopped for Candy; it's reversed. A plastic surgeon could not have altered her features more profoundly. She is in the witness protection program. That must be it.

— I saw your light.

She speaks! Her voice, almost masculine in tone, is hesitant, as if we're strangers.

— I knew you'd make it.

— The end to a totally weird journey.

— The important thing is you're here at last. I've got so many questions.

— Would it be okay if we went to the house now? I'm really beat.

— I was only out here to guide you.

— Hold on one second, would you? I'm dying.

She moves to the edge of the rock, unzips her pants and sends a stream of urine onto the ground.

— You're a man.

— Don't you start. You don't even know me.

Something's not right.

— Who the fuck are you?

— Take it easy, man. I'm looking for my mother.

No, this is not Candy, but a strange young man. He lacks the requisite toughness to be a biker. Turning from the empty road at the tempting flicker of hope. There's only room for one obsessed guy in the Wasteland at a time.

— You found mine instead, and you just pissed all over her grave. I suggest you retrace your steps and watch out for the quicksand.

The kid backs away without the grace and sultriness of Molly O. A silhouette turns down the path, running into darkness, following the yellow rope to safety. Maybe I should not have mentioned the quicksand. I think sometimes that only those who believe in it have to worry.

I feel impotent, incapable of crawling back in the dark against a malevolent environment. Best to keep vigil on the rock.

ANTHEA STANDS AT the frying pan, her back to me.

— I think we need to process what happened last night.

I stare, bleary-eyed and stiff from a night contracting my muscles to protect myself against the cold and the frogs.

What part of last night does she mean?

— I was upset about Hoss disappearing. He's still not back. But I realize this is a difficult time for you. I don't want to be a burden.

She turns the pancakes over and sniffles.

— Sorry I threw the bracelet. I had no right to go through those clothes or try on the perfume. I don't know what came over me.

— Don't believe her, man. She's always going through my drawers.

— Swann! I told you to wait upstairs.

Anthea is blushing now. Her voice, which sounds less hoarse this morning, is dry again.

— I'm sorry, LJ. First me, now my son too. We're taking up so much space in your moment of grief. It's just that Swann needs a lot of looking after, and ...

The smoke alarm cuts through the bullshit with piercing beeps. Anthea rushes to the stove to take the pan off the burner. In her haste, one of the pancakes slides onto the floor. It sits there while she catches her breath and Swann removes the battery from the alarm. He scans the kitchen for her purse, finds the puffer on his first thrust into the deep chasm and puts an arm around her shoulders as she inhales deeply.

The whole place could be vacuumed to suck up the dust and cobwebs, all traces of neglect. I wonder if Candy has allergies or if her immune system, like the rest of her, has remained totally uncompromised. She could stand in the middle of the ozone layer and not get burnt. Or so I believed.

31

AN AIRPLANE IS GETTING LOUDER and closer. I leave Swann and Anthea with their pancakes and run to the stage. What better re-entry into our lives than landing in a custom-made parachute with blazing colours. When she hits the ground, her gas mask will protect her from the toxic fumes. Such drama! Such poetry! I'm turning into a bad screenwriter.

I crane my neck, waiting for the plane to make a second pass. No joy.

— I don't think it's coming back.

His voice, apart from the masculine timbre, is so much like what I imagine Candy's will be like, if she talks. New. Elegant.

— Sometimes they write messages with the smoke.

— A stage in the middle of the country is the perfect set-up. I've got a telescope back home, you know.

— The words can be miles long. If there's no wind, they can hover up there quite a while.

— I want to discover a new star or something. Is that crazy?

— A bunch of planes fly in formation. They release smoke in sequence. I've read about it. Skywriting.

— Last night, after I ran away from you, I lay on the stage for an hour. Comet Swann. How cool is that?

I'm not surprised Candy hasn't taken up skydiving. She has typically gravitated towards the earth. That ostensibly solid ground could turn and swallow a person whole has always captivated and frightened her. On auction nights, while we set up, she would gaze into the Wasteland. Did she mouth a prayer or a curse? She would walk backwards on the stage not just to control the gaze of the patrons, but also to keep the spectre of the dead field out of sight and, paradoxically, to take strength from it.

Those nights we crawled under the stage might have been the most powerful influence of all on her creation of Molly O. This was where it all began: sitting in the dark, with the boards bowing under Joseph's weight, his chants spawning with dirt to enter our pores, the cool air from the Wasteland flowing into our secret lair from the south. We experienced elusive intimacy.

No way could I cram myself in there again with or without Candy. I'll walk on the boards above her head. There and not there. So close, so far.

— It's like three giant lily pads. I've never seen a stage like this. Did you have an orchestra playing here? I've been accepted into Cornish this fall. It's the best music school in Seattle. They can wait. It's La Scala or bust for me.

— Your mother tore up the front of it.

— The Queen Mother did that?

— I was stuck underneath.

— I'm not a snob, you know. I might even sing in cabarets and clubs.

— You didn't see the sign out front under the big "G"? We held auctions here. Big ones.

— You've seen *Citizen Kane*, right? He had a big "K" on his fence.

— Kubla Khan. We generally call our property the Wasteland, which can refer to the field behind you, the house, the stage, or all three. Depends how people feel in the moment.

— You're not into this "moment" shit too, are you? My mother's such a head case. I can't let her out of my sight. Not for a minute.

— Which is why you left your father's house. To take care of your mother.

— He lent me the bike. I hid it in the barn.

— So are you going to help me fix this stage?

SWANN STARES AT me, his blue eyes mirrors. His blond hair is luxuriously thick and unfashionably long. His voice, featherlight. He saws boards with the drama of a magician cutting a woman in half. Slow, deliberate strokes, as if a life depended on it.

— You crawl under the stage. You sit on a rock all night. You stare into the sky waiting for words. Sorry about your mother's grave.

— Can't you talk and saw boards at the same time?

The boards don't match in size, shape, or colour, but a hole has been covered, the sanctity of the hiding place restored.

Candy will appreciate the effort, if not the half-assed result.

Swann is whirling around on the second tier of the stage in the bright sunlight, a blur of flinging hair.

— I thought you were an opera singer.

— I try to be *l'artiste absolu* — singer, dancer, poet, magician.

He does the splits, then lifts himself back up with two fingers.

— I thought an opera singer needed heft.

— What's wrong with dreaming?

— Nothing. You can be the It Boy.

— I'm not sure the Wasteland likes me up here.

— Don't look at the field. Try moving around backwards.

— Like an eclipse. I get it.

Swann's heels brush up against the steps. As if jolted by electricity, he boomerangs back to centre stage. He stumbles wildly across the surface, arms flailing. A mysterious force carries him right to the edge. His arms push out into nothingness as he desperately tries to right himself. He's right on the spot where Hoss fell.

— Look out!

I leap closer, arms out, abs braced. How heavy can this kid be?

He winks! His right arm turns from a flail into a casual wave in my direction. He pulls his chest even with the rest of his body and falls backwards on his hands in the middle of the stage. He transforms his routine into a short breakdance before leaping to the third tier in a single bound.

Candy could never do any of this. Maybe Swann would teach her.

I lie on the boards with one ear attuned to any movement underneath, and the opposite eye on Swann, whose prancing on the stage comes regularly into my peripheral vision.

32

— SOMETIMES HE'S A HAPPY SEVEN, but at night he calls out in his sleep so I think he's a fearful Six. I want him to do an Enneagram retreat so I can know how to parent him better. He is so fixated on opera. You know how many times a day I listen to that?

Through the open kitchen window, I can hear Swann singing a strange warm-up exercise in the barn. It's not a song, exactly, although it has rhythm. The kitsch-happy hohoho and lalala seem from another time.

— "I'm Glad I Am Finally Going Home." That's what it's called. It's some Russian thing that was all the rage on YouTube.

Maybe Candy will give us a rollicking rendition of her own.

Anthea has set up *The Riflemen* on the kitchen table. Initially an auction leftover for rainy days, the board game is now helping kill a sunny one since Anthea won't risk getting burned outside. Candy liked to take on the identity of the father, Lucas McCain, leaving me to play Mark, the son. Roll, spin, and move. She always managed to get her herd of cattle into the opposite corral first. What's taking her so long to get home this time?

— Ashok is a truly kind and wise man. He knows a lot about you now. At least from what Janardan has said about your family. He wants to meet you one day.

— I'm not interested in answers, only questions.

Not true. If Ashok has an inside track on Candy's whereabouts, I'll bray like a donkey and he can pin any number he wants on my ass.

— Just being in his presence lifts the weight from your heart. He's funny, too. Spirituality doesn't have to be serious. I learned that from Ashok. He doesn't play favourites either, not like some other teachers I've had. He loves us all equally.

— I thought you were pissed at him for switching your number.

— I let it go.

— Don't believe anything Hoss says about me when he's under the influence of a guru.

— It takes a great deal of reflection for him to decide who you are. I have to take my share of responsibility. I'm internally inconsistent.

The doorknob turns on the back screen door, and my heart jumps a little. All my fantasies have revolved around Candy using the front door. So what? I'm open to change.

— It still works, man! Come see! Quick, Mom. The sun's under a cloud.

I need to hang bells around Swann's ankles so I recognize his tread. I don't like the idea of him touching the Steenbeck. The last time it was up and running Candy was still appearing on our stage. It's sacrilegious to play with its rollers and reels.

As we cross the yard, Anthea touches my arm and pulls me down to whisper in my ear.

— He stole his father's motorcycle. I should have left him at home.

Swann heads directly to Flicker, whose dust cloth lies in a heap on the ground. He pops in a quarter and sends a ball cascading through the faces of early Hollywood. He racks up points on the board, and the numbers add normally and don't change. Lights flash, but bells and whistles also chime with each bounce off the bumper or target. For the first time ever at the Wasteland, Flicker is firing on all cylinders. Either Joseph tinkered with the wiring or the machine repaired itself. I am terribly confused, but stand ready to lay a laurel wreath as tribute.

— Swann! It's a pinball machine, not the Second Coming.

Neither can appreciate the significance of Flicker's rebirth. If this small miracle, unexpected and unasked for, can transpire in our humble barn, what might be possible from all the energy I've expended on willing Candy back to the fold. I'm thinking like an Ashok disciple, convinced the universe is not indifferent but sending signals to those who can read them.

33

I KEEP WONDERING HOW A quick stop to the pharmacy for sunscreen could have delayed them so long. Was Anthea searching for the right mix of shea butter and aloe vera? But no, there is more to the story. Hoss must have warned her about the state of our larder, and she insisted on stopping at the bulk food store. But for the legumes, they might have got here before Joseph died. On the first night she left her lentils in the cupboard out of politeness, but she feels at home now. For the first time since crops were harvested in our fields, centuries ago, the table is brimming with natural goodness. So healthy I choke just to look at it.

Swann bounds down the stairs, wide-eyed.

— Man, you should charge admission to that room. All those long-playing records.

— Swann! You didn't play LJ's music!

— Don't worry. There was a box of surgical gloves. I didn't catch anything.

I like this kid.

— And the *Playboys*. With a Canadian playmate! She was so hot. But she must be, like, sixty now. How weird is that. Downright creepy, man. Can't you get your kicks online like everyone else?

— Swann! I'm sure LJ has a reason for keeping pornography in the house. It's none of our business. And stay out of the girl's bedroom.

Anthea and Swann both go quiet, embarrassed for me. As if I can't stomach the idea that we're talking about Candy behind her back. No, they feel the need to protect my feelings, which is worse.

— I hope you kept the gloves on while you looked at the centrefold.

— I could not even get the pages to lift and separate, man. They are positively glued shut.

— Can we stop with the juvenile jokes? It's been twenty-four hours. Is it normal that Janardan would leave like this and then not call?

— Those are my brother's records.

Given Swann's lapse into thoughtful silence, Hoss has moved up a notch in his estimation. I didn't realize they'd even met. Yet they seem to have a history. One more relationship for me to circumnavigate.

— I took Swann to see Jon Anderson last year. He didn't understand a word.

— Didn't matter. The guy could shatter glass.

— Swann wants to sing. Like his father. I thought they'd connect over music.

— He still listens to Donovan. *Patetico!*

— You know Yes fired Jon Anderson and hired an avatar? Someone younger who sounds just like him. Then Ian Anderson hired an avatar for himself to sing the high parts for the *Thick as a Brick* sequel. They think they can stop time. They're not accepting life in the moment.

How long has Hoss been standing there? He is glowing. It's not often he can integrate arcane prog-rock knowledge and nuggets of spiritual wisdom into everyday conversation so easily. But he should not push too hard against living in the past. This is someone who owns the complete collection of *Bonanza* on one hundred and thirteen DVDs.

— I've brought someone special with me.

My fingers, tacky with wholesome nutrients, grip the Formica. A few AWOL navy beans are lodged in my throat. All I can do is glare. Choosing Hoss over me? I am not her Orpheus, destined to escort Eurydice back to the land of the living, the first to see her again. Unless she's held me in reserve for a larger purpose. The way, in credits, the most important actor often appears last. My fingers regain dexterity, food passes into my esophagus. But Anthea beats me to the indignant response.

— Where the fuck have you been?

— Yeah, where the fuck?

— Swann!

Hoss seems to notice Swann for the first time, this blond upstart in his chair.

— I was dealing with the undertaker and the lawyer.

"Undertaker" is a Joseph kind of word, imbedded in

another era. I'm impressed with Hoss's diction and self-control, the way he sucks the righteousness right out of Anthea with this oblique reference to our recent loss. Who could recover from such a low blow?

Round and around on the back roads, marking time without a trace of Anthea's eco-consciousness. I know it's me Candy can't face. She wants to explain her life with a shrug and knows I'll never accept it. Not after I've brought her back through the blog. You needn't say it all out loud! Write a book. Maybe make a sequel to *Going, going, gone*. I could help. No hard feelings.

She's in the car, collecting her thoughts, gathering her courage. This homecoming is more intense than she has imagined. The dam of grief has burst. A lifetime of long-forgotten tears flows down her cheeks. She doesn't notice how quickly they fill up the car, threatening to short-circuit the electrical systems. By the time my hands, sticky from quinoa, pull at the locked doors and pound on the closed windows, the salty water is up to her neck. With the very axe that rescued me from the crypt, I smash in a rear window. Water gushes out, carrying Candy on a wave into my arms.

Hoss moves quickly to block my rescue attempt. I bang up against some canned goods in the grocery bag. Frozen food is suddenly not good enough for my brother? It has to be some vegetable from Green Giant. Because even as I wince from the whack on my knee, the blow has opened a long-lost file of TV commercials in my brain, and the giant's "Ho, Ho, Ho" starts playing in a loop. I used to like the jingle. Now I think the giant is laughing at me.

— Our guest doesn't want to be disturbed. He's preparing. He's taking it all in.

Hoss thinks a masculine pronoun will throw me off the scent? He forgets that Candy belongs to no one. Not even me. The insight makes me limp back to my chair. Swann brings me a Hungry Man Dinner as an icepack.

— You brought someone *speziale*. Like we care, man. You hurt your brother.

Swann grins slyly at me. Candy will like him.

— You bring me and then leave. I'm not *speziale* enough? I thought we had a connection.

Another asthma attack can't be far off.

— Yes, I brought someone special. Period. No comment.

He plants the bags on the counter and pulls out the items, his back towards us. With a deep breath, he appears to be debating whether to store things in the cupboard or send them flying. He adjusts to what's needed, faces us with a look of superior wisdom.

— You are where you need to be.

— You think I need to be in this lunatic asylum?

— What she said, man.

— Swann!

— Our guest wants some time alone before coming inside the house. He is attuning to the propitious moment. Is that so much to ask?

A refugee, internally displaced or eternally expected, but hardly a guest. I know she's perusing the yard, walking across the tiers of the stage, inspecting the barn. I wish she'd hurry up. I need a package of frozen Buffalo chicken for my forehead because the room is spinning and I can't handle another disappointment.

 — I'm sorry to be the cause of so much consternation.

34

IF I HAVE SPENT MY adult life grasping for Candy at every turn, our sister has never ranked high on Hoss's inner search engine. His spiritual path brooks no detours. It flows one way, optimized to ignore fresh breadcrumbs, hidden code, or promising links. In Hoss's narrow, moment-based world, Candy could never be special. She is too far beyond established perimeters to register in his consciousness. I know this, or should. So why do I feel utterly drained? Hoss has taken a can opener to my heart, ripped the lid off my hopes and poured them down the sink like so much dirty lentil rinse water.

Hoss seems to have hauled a long-haired, bearded, and generally unkempt Ian Anderson off the stage of a Jethro Tull concert circa 1970 in the midst of singing "Back to the Family." He's kept the flute, but replaced the patchwork hand-me-downs with an embroidered cotton shirt and knitted cap, and given him the complexion of an East Indian, an East European accent, and another foot in height.

— Ashok!

Anthea jumps up to give him a hug that lasts about four seconds longer than I would call normal. He waves to Hoss, who has put down his can of Niblets on the counter out of respect. He smiles broadly at Swann, who looks back coldly. Turning to me, with a self-satisfied twinkle in his eye, Ashok says:

— I must be a shock to you.

— Not really. Do you know any Jann Arden tunes?

— Please excuse my brother. I warned you.

— Actually, could you excuse both of us? I'd like to talk to Hoss in private.

— I'm quite happy to wander around outside.

— Be sure to take a walk in the field. It's the highlight of any trip to the Wasteland.

Ashok laughs.

— I like you, Little Joe. I hope we'll have a chance to talk, just the two of us.

— I'll have my people call your people.

I'm sure Hoss has told Ashok all about my quicksand fixation. How it's one more fantasy from the past that I cling onto. How the field may be desolate and toxic, but remains essentially harmless to the casual traveller, even during spring storms. Boots have never been known to sink lower than ankles in the muck. We'll see who's right.

Swann heads upstairs, while Anthea gives Hoss a haughty look before slipping out the back door with Ashok.

— So you brought your guru.

— Teacher.

— It wasn't enough to bring your girlfriend and her son, and then leave them with me.

— You are so wrong, as usual. I've got a lot done, so can you drop the attitude? I can't stay in this kitchen. The energy is oppressive. Let's go for a walk.

My knee is throbbing from its collision with the can of corn, but I won't give Hoss the satisfaction of seeing how much he's hurt me. Anyway, he doesn't notice the limp because he keeps two strides ahead.

THERE IS, APPARENTLY, an arcane New Age law that says the eldest child is fated for certain tasks. Hoss remembers this from a birth-order workshop with Ashok. So it makes perfect sense to him that he has been named executor of the estate. Never mind his early failure and defection, the sparse visits to the Wasteland, the lifetime of avoiding any discussion about Candy. I think Joseph wants to punish him and spare me the hassle of the paperwork. He certainly doesn't want to saddle Candy with the burden — not on her first day back home.

Hoss has made arrangements, as one assembles flowers in a vase. Joseph does not want us wasting our inheritance. The will is clear on this point and Hoss is determined to respect our father's wishes. Not something he'd ever done while Joseph was alive, but death changes everything.

Only two times are available each day for families wishing to witness the cremation of their loved one. Hoss books the early morning slot tomorrow. He'll pick up the ashes the following day. We'll spread them in the Wasteland that afternoon. They're calling for sun.

The heavy chest, bowed head, and general stupor are yesterday's moment. Buoyed by the arrival of his guru, he strides along the concession road with a spring in his step. His dust in my face clouds my thinking. My plan has always been to present the film montage of Candy and Molly O, and evidence from my blog, at the right moment. What does it matter if Hoss believes me or not? It just does. But he will sit after watching my film with a smug and superior look, the kind he once got from Genesis. He won't dare express an opinion before his guru, and Ashok will dismiss my logic out of hand. To accept Candy's career as Molly O throws everything into question, including Hoss's commitment to Momentous Moments. Ashok will not release his followers without a fight. It may take Candy herself to cut his stranglehold over Hoss. No one can seduce like she can. Her arrival will free us all. I only need give her enough time to find the blog and get here. If I think it quickly enough, it almost sounds possible.

— What's the rush? You don't want to stay in this moment a while, read up on the Tibetan Book of the Dead?

— We're leaving on Friday. We need to think about how to clean out the house and sell the place.

Typical Hoss. Make a plan that's impossible for him to execute. For once his hypocrisy may end in my favour. If Candy doesn't show right away, I can work with a real estate agent and make sure the place doesn't sell. I won't have Candy return to a different family at the Wasteland, or worse, an empty lot. Nor will I hire Cyril McInnis to stand on our stage and auction off all our useless and unsellable heir-looms. But making the Wasteland unsellable is Plan B. In the meantime, Candy will surely arrive. Maybe she'll want to buy the Wasteland to keep it in the family. She can have my share.

— On second thought, better keep the furniture. For now. Empty houses are harder to sell. We should just clean out the clutter.

— I remind you the estate has been divided into three equal parts. Joseph clearly thinks we should track Candy down. I have some —

— Will you stop talking in the present tense? He's dead. So is she. The lawyer says death *in absentia* is just a formality after all these years.

— All these years of what?

Hoss can't say Candy's name, and doesn't seem to mind.

— You've been *in absentia* from the Wasteland most of your adult life, and yet you seem to be among the living. The three of us need to agree on what to do next.

— There is no three. There is you and me. I'm glad Ashok is here. I hope you'll learn from him.

— About that. What the fuck?

— I need him here. Hear me out, would you?

Hoss stops abruptly in front of Rox's house, too self-absorbed to notice the bus shelter is gone. It's normal for the wooden floor to have extinguished all life underneath by now. But there's no dry splotch of earth, not even a square of dead flattened grass. It's as if the shelter has never been. In an echo of some B-grade horror movie, the weeds that had ensnarled Candy's words have taken back the land. Frogs can't be far behind. No sooner do I discover a piece of Candy unknown to me than it disappears. Has my intrusion released a plague of locusts that devoured the wood? Pestilence, wild animals, flies, blood — what's next? If Candy is enslaved in Egypt, let her go before her absence ruins us all.

— When I took off the other night, I drove to the Night Brew. It was a real lapse into my old self. I wanted to score some weed. It's a parking lot now.

— They paved paradise.

— Will you shut up for two minutes?

When haven't I listened to Hoss? All those early mornings back from Shep with the munchies, shaking me awake so he could recap the excellent weed, the good deals, the bad girls, while showering my face with bits of chocolate from his Jos. Louis cakes.

— I spent hours driving around my old haunts, looking at punks making deals. I could have stayed a loser like them. But I grew, as a person. I developed. I haven't smoked in years.

I'm not sure if his voice is cracking with emotion or late-breaking adolescence. I notice his paunch and greying hair for the first time. When did my brother get so much older?

— I bought some weed from a girl. We smoked together. She was maybe seventeen. She had Crimson on her iPod, the fortieth anniversary edition of *Larks' Tongues in Aspic*. Fifteen discs. Live recordings, alternate takes, remixes. Bootlegs rediscovered and remastered. We were listening in tandem through earphones. This was the girl of my fucking dreams, and I'd met her thirty-five years too late. I wasn't sure if we were having a moment together or if she was just bored. I quoted from "Exiles." Except I said the palm of my hand was "wet" instead of "damp." She laughed in my face.

Hoss must be in a bad way to forget Crimson lyrics and then openly admit it to me. He looks at me plaintively, probably the same way he stood before Ashok to confess his forbidden relations at the retreat. Either he wants more punishment or absolution. The truth is, while Bootleg Girl is demeaning Hoss with her wet talk, Authentic Girl is dousing herself with Perrier to humiliate me. Maybe we're not so unalike. We're both looking for Candy in all the wrong places.

— Wet, damp, moist, clammy, it's only talk.

A lame reference to another Crimson song, but enough for Hoss to offer a slight smile. He turns for home, his stride less confident. The soothing effect of Ashok's influence has a limited range, and he needs a recharge. Maybe we should stay parked out here on the third. I like him like this, sidetracked from his spiritual path, floundering with uncertainty. It makes me feel older.

— I came to see Joseph last year. I wanted to ease his suffering, send a few waves of energy to build up his reserves. He'd fallen asleep with the light on. It took me ten minutes to move closer to the bed. The covers were off. He was lying there in pyjamas, all exposed, snoring. I could not get my hands to move. They weren't on fire, just heavy. Damp, in fact. Holy fuck. Just like in the song. That's what it means. That's what it's all about. I was exiled from myself.

— Sure.

— I'm standing in Joseph's room and the moon appears from behind a cloud. There's a moon on the cover of *Larks' Tongues in Aspic*. I am freaking out.

— There's a sun on the cover, too.

— Remember that episode of *M*A*S*H* when the power goes out, and they move all the wounded out of the operating room into the field, and Radar orders a fleet of trucks to shine their headlights so the doctors can see? It was like that. A flash of inspiration, a flash of light. Joseph seemed at peace. I forgave him everything and I asked for his forgiveness. Nothing I could articulate. It was just a feeling. I felt clean on the inside. My hands were lighter. They were dry. Without trying, I had attuned to my innermost needs and reached a decision. I would offer my gift of healing, such as it was, and risk his rejection. Maybe I would do some good. Maybe I wouldn't. I had no ulterior motives. It was coming from a place of unconditional love. Then the moon disappeared and he turned his fucking back on me.

He's expecting a snide comment, but I actually wish he could stay in these moments of despair, however impure, instead of running to the guru for love.

— Ashok can help us get through this. Give him a chance. You won't even notice him. He'll sleep on the stage. He likes a hard surface. They're calling for clouds, but no rain.

— We don't need him. Candy is coming home.

Molly O
The seductive cinema of Mickey Nailand

| Home | Films | Suppositions | About Me |

Molly O, this is your moment!
Posted by LJ

When Mickey Nailand dies, Molly O apparently enters a self-imposed exile from which she has never released herself. Perhaps, rather than wearing a black veil all these years for her soulmate and creative partner, she has been biding her time. Her films with Nailand garnered small audiences at alternative venues. They could easily have vanished forever. Yet someone arranges to deposit not just the films but also the scripts and production notes to the Film-makers' Cooperative in New York. Molly O does not want their work forgotten. Nor will it be. A complete retrospective of Nailand's films in New York is planned. What better moment for Molly O to resurface and guide a reconsideration of her work.

Molly O, wherever you are, now is your moment. Emerge from the shelter you've erected around yourself. Assume your rightful place alongside Mary Pickford, Theda Barra, Louise

Brooks, and the rest of the pantheon. Reconnect with your past before all this precious heritage becomes a wasteland.

Leave a comment

35

IN THE WORLD'S FIRST FILM, in 1895, the Lumière brothers document workers pouring out of their factory in Lyon for forty-six seconds. It will take a few more years before Méliès depicts a spaceship landing in the moon's right eye. Magic and poetry have been at war with the conventions of realism ever since. I am with Maurice Pialat on this — realism is for other people. What I feel is close to faith. Candy will see my message. She will understand it. She will come.

36

HOSS PICKS UP THE PACE and, with my knee still smarting from its contact with the Green Giant, I can't keep up. By the time I limp back into the Wasteland, he's nowhere in sight. Anthea and Ashok sit on the porch as if they belong here, while Swann is back in the barn singing his Russian "Ho, Ho, Ho" song. Any second now, the giant himself will join in.

Anthea won't let me pass unheeded into the house.

— You really upset Janardan. He locked himself in the bedroom and won't answer the door.

— He's probably wearing headphones.

— He's a completely different person here.

— He needs some space.

My attempt to sound like Hoss is patently false, and she knows it. She marches into the house for another shot at changing Hoss back into Janardan. Maybe, like the region code of a DVD player in a computer, you can only switch so many times before you have to choose where, or who, you want to be.

Ashok motions to the empty chair beside him.

— You're hurting.

— My soul?

— Your knee.

I can't bring myself to appear weak in front of the guru so I stand there, putting weight on my other leg.

— Maybe I can help. I have some experience with reiki.

— All I need is more frozen food to bring the swelling down. You could put some Buffalo wings on that big head of yours. It might help you, too.

— I know you feel threatened by my presence.

— I don't believe in the medicine you're offering. You've turned Hoss inside out.

— Sometimes, when washing delicate clothing, you turn it inside out to protect the outer layer.

— Brainwashing is a delicate operation, I grant you that. You've got to separate the whites from the grey matter. One weekend of sculpting on an island, and you're an expert on my family.

— Many weekends with me, and many years with other people. You don't know your brother as well as you think. He's been trying to heal from the loss of Candy for a long time. He'd been making progress. This weekend was an important piece. Then came the news of your father's death, and — how would you call it? — the flare that you sent up today about your sister.

— I think the expression you're looking for is "the bombshell I dropped."

— I hate to see Janardan in pain, and given false hope. He

was coming into a new phase of acceptance about the loss through the family sculpting.

— We'll see what's false and what's true.

I'M SURE ANTHEA'S heart-rending performance of Candy brought the house down at the retreat, but I keep wondering how I was depicted in this family sculpture. Maybe Hoss just had some guy stand two years behind him and look over the horizon with a mournful countenance. A non-speaking part so I couldn't challenge his healing path away from Candy. Have I been foolishly holding on to our sister all these years when, with a few well-placed handfuls of gooey self-help clay, I could have reshaped the mould that binds me? Away from the smug Ashok and the self-righteous Hoss, I can admit there is not much to go on. Yes, I believe my analysis of the Nailand films is sound, but there's no reason to think Candy is coming. Not today, not next week. But no reason not to believe either.

A FEW HOURS after miraculously producing all manner of buzzes, twangs, and whistles, Flicker falls silent. Swann is convinced that one more tilt, bump, or slap will bring back the sound. Who am I to suggest otherwise? Eventually he gives up, at least for now, and wanders aimlessly around the barn.

— I should get this bike back to my dad soon, except I'm afraid to leave my mother alone. This Ashok is one scary dude, man. Most of the time she gets tired of "a new spiritual path" by now. Roadkill, you know? But she really believes in this guy. Or she's in love with your brother. If they get married, what does that make us?

— I wish you'd hang out here a while longer.

— Hang, man. No one says "hang out" anymore.

How will I survive the Wasteland without him? He's an iconoclast, a free thinker. He'll see my film about Candy and Molly O and start baking a cake.

— Ashok has got a wanking big-screen TV in his basement. This guy is loaded. Although why anyone would want to live in Hamilton. No offence, man. When she gets home from one of his retreats, I have to pull my mother off the ceiling. Nonstop talking. A play-by-play of every frickin' moment. Three days later, she calls in sick. She's still in bed when I get home from school. What will happen when I'm in La Scala?

Anthea wanders into the barn, arms crossed for warmth or self-love. This place used to be a sanctuary. Now it's a crossroads.

— Can you beetle off, Swann?

— You folks want to hang out for a while, huh?

He pats Flicker on his way out. With affection or impatience it's hard to say.

— Janardan is morose. Everything in the retreat has been undone. Stay in the moment, but when it's so full of pain, who needs it? I organized a retreat in Buffalo last year. I found a nice place, not too expensive. Nothing fancy. Not like this island that Jackie booked that Ashok couldn't shut up about. I wanted to be noticed. It's part of being a Four, needing to be special. Nothing. No special looks, no unique moments. He never once came to my house. But he comes here, totally out of the way. Where does that leave me?

— Talking to the wind.

— How about you and I have a conversation? I don't understand what's happening with your sister. She's really coming back?

How tempting to share my deepest hopes and fears with this strange creature from Buffalo. Set her down at the Steenbeck and recount the evolution of *Going, going, gone*. Bring her up to the auction stage and regale her with anecdotes from Candy's performances. Test my theories about Molly O, and show her my blogs. Except I don't trust her to respond positively. And, no, I don't trust myself to get the words out right. Stick to Plan A. Show my film in a controlled setting. After we get back from the cremation, unless Candy beats me to the punch.

37

THE WHITE CHALK MARKS HAVE lost some of their substance over three decades. Specks of black have appeared in the middle of the letters. One time Joseph lost his balance and rubbed the fine definition off the "r." It might have been worse, but he steered himself to the floor rather than wipe out the words. Despite all odds, the message has survived. On visits home, my eyes invariably stray to "Rx. Later" and it comforts me.

But our father is dead, the blackboard and felt brush are part of his effects and Hoss has the power to execute. He waves the brush at me, gesticulating like a mad scientist about to wipe out a mathematical formula that will save the world.

— Don't!

— She is not coming back. In this world or the next. Later or ever. Keeping it up there all these years has been a prescription for madness.

Do I detect a slight East European accent by way of southern Ontario emerging from Hoss's mouth? Ashok has pumped up Hoss with a seductive speech about letting go of the past and now my brother has launched a jihad against Candy.

I leap towards him, but he's already moved a step closer. The brush hovers perilously close to the words.

— One more step and these words are history.

— History is never over. It gets reinterpreted and it changes. You could never see that.

Swann starts moving towards Hoss. With my brother distracted, I take another giant leap to pull his arm away. I don't have enough leverage to dislodge the brush from his hand. All I can do now is keep him from using it, and lock up his other hand with mine. The fibres of the brush are breathing on the board and then I pull us away again. Heat from Hoss's hand starts to tingle my palm. It won't be long before I get third-degree burns. We're stuck in this dance with no way out.

— You can't even say her name.

— Candy! Candy!

The sound of Hoss's excited voice makes me think our sister is right behind me. I let up my grip for a second to check over my shoulder and we both go down, dislodging the blackboard. Anthea helps Hoss to his feet, while Swann helps me gather the broken pieces.

— Saying her name like that. You've taken another step forward on the path.

Ashok is not worried about setting Caine and Abel at their

throats, only at leading his disciple down the garden path. If Candy is blocking his way, push her into the sea. Is allowing Candy the right to exist so much to ask?

WHILE I LIE on Candy's bed, Swann assembles shards of slate on the floor. Some of them are tiny slivers, while others resemble a slice of pizza. He looks for white amid the black, without asking why the words are worth fighting for.

— Rx like prescription?

— It's short for Rox, her best friend.

— It also stands for chemical reaction.

All these years of assuming I understand what Rx means only to discover I'm missing the obvious. By "chemical reaction" is she predicting a fiery connection with Mickey Nailand or simply telling us about the love flowing through her system? Either way, it changes the meaning of "later." It's no longer merely a promise to return home, but rather a prescient recognition of the ephemeral nature of passion. Or maybe my brain cells are addled, too, and it just means "Rox" like it always did. It's all good. New possibilities feed my hopes.

— I've never been to a funeral before. Is there singing?

— You'll need to ask my brother. He's in charge.

— Is Ashok going to say something?

— Over my dead body.

Swann rolls towards the bed, exhausted, coming to rest about where Rox would sleep with Candy. I don't know if it's the room, that I'm lying on my back, or that I can't see Swann's face, but words start pouring out. I tell him all about

Candy before she disappeared. I leave out my discovery and theories of Molly O. Plan A is still in force.

Growing shadows block out the peeling paint on the walls. Which is fine. I prefer to remember the room pristine, as it once was. Distant thunder. The heavens are saying I was wrong to disturb the silence.

— Keep looking for her, man.

We lie without speaking, undisturbed until a tiny rap on the door signals the arrival of two plates of tofu-vegetable stir-fry on a bed of kasha. Neither of us eats or moves.

— Can I look at Phebe's things?

— They're gone.

Spirited away or taken by Rox before she left. He looks anyway, shining Candy's desk lamp into the corner. Prying up the loose board, he reaches into empty space.

— I feel something.

I turn my head to face the wall.

— Check this out! There's an old photo, a lock of hair ...

I roll over so quickly that I tumble onto the floor. Avoiding the slate pieces so precisely arranged, I crawl towards Swann on all fours. It is Phebe's cache, restored to its proper place. Was it there the whole time? Far away, so close. My hands tremble holding these treasures. I scan the blank pages for a sign of black letters, convinced that maybe even her words have reappeared. If not, there's always tomorrow.

From the window, I see Hoss set up a bed for Ashok on the stage. If Candy does make it back before dawn, she will stumble first upon the Hungarian from Hamilton. She may depart without a word or do him an injury for invading her space. I need to be a countervailing force in the field. This time I will make sure the flashlight batteries work, and my beacon will guide her home.

I gaze at the hundreds of pieces from the broken message board Swann has grouped into slate black and chalk white. No skywriting, only clouds and smoke. My hand moves a few white pieces around and then a few more, as if guided by a Ouija board. The shapes hint at letters and I switch pieces feverishly until I uncover an unmistakable sign from Candy.

"late."

My fever doesn't let up. My head hurts. Because I can also see "tale."

The sign is mistakable, after all, and I'm not sure which of my narratives about Candy to believe anymore.

38

I SPREAD NOTES FOR CANDY all over the house, urging her to meet us at the funeral home by eight. The others have gone ahead. I drive slowly along the concession road, checking behind for a figure waving at me madly to stop. Candy. Joseph. Mary. Anyone would do. But no one's on this desolate road but me. Not even Rox has come back in time.

I can't tear my eyes off the rear-view mirror. So much so that I narrowly miss a large rock dead ahead. The past is more compelling than the present. Has it come to this? No, it's been like this a while.

Garish armchairs tucked into every nook and cranny, dark coffee tables empty of mugs or cups, insipid paintings of birds in flight or flowers on sedate walls. A solemn young man in a poorly cut suit motions with his arm to follow him down the corridor.

— Are you expecting anyone else?

— Possibly.

— We can wait a few more minutes. After, you can stay as long as you like.

— Until the last credit rolls and the curtain falls.

He's never thought of the viewing room as a film theatre, but smiles blankly, accustomed to mourners and their strange ways. He doesn't know the half of it.

Hoss, Anthea, and Ashok are sitting cross-legged under a shuttered picture window, eyes closed, bodies rocking as they chant the same indecipherable words over and over. Swann has saved me a seat, needlessly since the others aren't going anywhere, but I appreciate the gesture nevertheless. Then I see the plastic baggie of jujubes that safeguards the third seat. Nice touch. He has understood even without me saying. In the Candy wars, he is my aide-de-camp.

HOSS SCRAMBLES TO his feet, bends over, and hugs me awkwardly. The sight of Ashok's smug face observing our brotherly reconciliation keeps me firmly planted in the chair. They're all on their feet now, standing in front of the window and blocking our view. This isn't a cinema for them, it's a rock concert, and they're obnoxious fans. Any moment now Hoss will flick his lighter and Anthea will start a ritual clap to bring out the main attraction. I've got one ear cocked to the door behind us, attuned to a delicate turn of the handle.

The blinds rise, revealing what looks like a large furnace duct connected to rollers that stand at waist level. A particle-board box sits on the rollers, a little off kilter. The rest of the room seems empty and sterile. It's hard to tell since we have no peripheral vision through the window. Ashok would say that all we can see is what's ahead of us. Candy, please hurry. Please.

The flickering green light and the horrendous racket coming from this machine don't inspire much confidence. Joseph's modest container will pass through an open flap, not the curtain I've seen in countless films. I only hope the green light doesn't go off halfway through, leaving him stuck in there.

The kid in the bad suit walks into the frame to adjust the machine. Without a glance at his audience, he positions the box and rolls it through the flap. It takes all of three seconds. He employs all the poise and poetry of a bagboy rolling groceries out the store to idling cars. My eyes are closed and I can see it all clearly: while we wait for our order to appear through the trap door, Joseph practises chants to the spin of the rollers and the thud of the plastic containers bumping into each other. Of course, the cars are never lined up in the same order as the groceries. I feel for the pimply kid outside in the cold, running up and down the row of cars, suffocating on fumes, getting honked at and pointed to, catching his own fingers between the plastic containers. He has a dignity the inside bagboy could never understand. My eyes well up with tears, overcome with nostalgia for car-pickup. Why must things change?

The three of them resume their positions on the floor and the two of us, not knowing what else to do, return to our chairs. I try to quench the hollowness in my gut with a handful of cherry jujubes.

— We are here to witness the last journey of Joseph Grant, Senior. His suffering on this earthly plane is now over.

— What the fuck does he know about Joseph's suffering and how the fuck does he know it's over? It's a two-part question.

— I thought you had discussed this with your brother. Perhaps I should leave.

— I'm making the decisions. I want you to stay.

Hoss pulls a lighter out of his pocket, and a ziplock bag with some mean-looking weed. He lights a clump, which emits a puff of smoke that smells illegal.

— Sage breeds purity.

He passes the herbs in front of Ashok and Anthea, waving the smoke into their faces and up and down the length of their bodies. She starts choking and reaches for her puffer. With an aggressive thrust, Hoss shoves the sage in our direction. I wave it away, but thick smoke now envelops the room, obscuring my brother from view. His defiant voice reaches me through an impenetrable haze.

— Ashok is buying the Wasteland.

From the ceiling, a smoke alarm emits a piercing beep. Hoss dumps the sage into a pitcher of water; Swann looks instinctively for a broom to clear the air; and Ashok closes his eyes calmly. On the other side of the window, the kid in the suit jumps into the frame to survey the oven. He throws us a dirty look, reaches for his cellphone, and lowers the blinds on our pagan smoke.

39

WE DIDN'T OWN HORSES OR cattle, not like the real family on *Bonanza*, but Joseph planted sagebrush every spring, out front near the archway and around the boulders. *Artemisia californica*. We lived in a kind of desert, so why not? It never took. The cactus died too. The ground was not fallow, just fucked-up. But I never stopped believing. Joseph was the wise patriarch. We were the loyal sons. The ones supposed to take over. It's not enough that he lost his wife and daughter, that we abandoned the family calling, that we haven't provided offspring. Now his firstborn wants to jettison our field of dreams to a guru with a big-screen TV. Ashok has never seen the *Bonanza* men burst through the burning map of the Ponderosa ranch on their horses in the opening of the show. But he wants to write our epilogue, removing us from the final credits. He's been salivating over the deed to our land. Spittle has rolled off his beard onto the page, his paw prints have smudged the wet spot and the name of Joseph Grant is barely legible.

He will purify the Wasteland of our family with his smart-ass sage, encircling that infernal weed over all our sacred places. His smoke will blacken the growth charts on the kitchen wall, make the *All My Children* tapes self-destruct in five seconds, cancel out Candy's scent from the bedroom. Never mind Joseph did not want sage tracked in the house.

He will take the house down altogether. No mercy. The driver will remove his hard hat. He'll breathe deeply with the rest of them before ramming the stones with his bulldozer. Rafters will tumble from the barn. Joists and two-by-fours will pummel the ancient Steenbeck. No moment of silence for *Going, going, gone*. He will keep the three-tiered stage for group meditations or mass marriages. The field will have to go. Drain the poison, fill up the quicksand, re-drill the well, bury the final resting places of Joseph and Mary. Don't forget the Wi-Fi for easy bank transfers. Plant your quinoa. I hope you choke on it.

I've been waiting so long. I don't have a right to be impatient? I suspect Candy has already arrived. She is devastated to hear news of Joseph's death, full of self-loathing for having missed the funeral by an hour. Even now, despite my many written reassurances, she debates whether she has the right to stay. But no, the concession road is calm, dust-free. No one has passed within the last hour. Not Rox, not Candy. Not even the others. Has my sister walked in from the highway? A whiff of doubt hovers on the passenger side. I lower the window before it can take hold.

They arrive, the four of them, after me. No Candy, but at least Hoss and Ashok have not waylaid her and forced her to sign off her third of the estate. The time has come to end this talk of death *in absentia* and selling the Wasteland, to show them that Candy is not just alive, but coming home. I only wish Rox were here for the show.

— Any talk of selling the Wasteland is premature. Everyone please sit. I have a short film to show you. It's silent so I will narrate. No questions until it's over.

A documentary film should respect the intelligence of its audience. It should raise questions, not provide answers. It should take the form of a meditative essay. No patronizing voiceovers to guide and direct the viewer. No commentary from the director before the actual screening. Better to allow people to experience the work on their own terms. Let them ask questions afterwards. Include an interview with the director in the special features of a DVD instead of a commentary plastered over the film.

But there is so little time and so much at stake. I can't afford for them to puzzle over my montage of auction film clips and classic Molly O scenes, to fill the gaps of silence with meaningless chatter. And so I stand next to the screen, professorially, about to sacrifice my beliefs for the higher good.

— There are good sightlines from the sofa. All right, on the floor if you must. Turn off your cellphones, please. Hit the lights, Swann. Candy gets her start in show business in our own backyard. She is a game show hostess here. Now she's Misty Rowe from *Hee Haw*. You see the bare feet? We did these commercials when we were kids. In high school there was a film club. Mr. Beecroft. He taught me how to develop 16 millimetre. The chemicals are slimy, hard to wash off. Here's Candy as Marlene Dietrich in *Shanghai Express*. As Theda Bara in *Cleopatra*. As Mary Pickford in *The Foundling*. The girl character is called Molly O. That's how I found her. Mary, Mickey, and Molly are the holy trinity. *One Hundred Percent American*. Look at the auctioneer's helper. Yes, exactly, an auctioneer. See how she moves backwards. Never looks behind, just like Candy on stage here. Mickey Nailand got into trouble with *M'liss*. You can hardly see her breasts. This is Nailand par excellence. Everything obscured, in shadow. See this guy in the front row without a bid card. That pork pie hat, it's the same one in this photo. The Buster Keaton look. Mickey Nailand. He was a mix of Dwoskin and early Fassbinder. But don't think Molly O was all his doing. Candy was the true genius. She invented Molly O. Of course she had to make silent films. What would you expect? The blackboards. Late. You can see the word on the floor upstairs. It's in *Mrs. Jones Entertains*, too. See the rubbed-off slate here? She said "later." She meant "late." You think Molly O is naked here, but look at the gloves. And here, and here. See the gloves? Mickey Nailand is the man who was bad. Sex. It's all through the films. But there is no porn. They are barely erotic. So much hidden. Like Candy, burying herself in Molly O. What you see is the depiction of absence. The inter-titles, the music, the shadows, they all conspire to keep us from Molly O. She remains elusive. Unable to be captured. A muse. I've started a blog and have printed off all my posts for you. I've sent her a coded message about Joseph. She didn't make it in time for the funeral.

But she's on her way. I'm pretty sure. In any case, we can't sell the Wasteland until she signs off her third of the estate.

It took all of fifteen minutes. If I had shown it days ago, when they first arrived, I could have avoided this unpleasantness with Hoss and Ashok. They would have understood the inappropriateness of real estate transactions. But I was waiting for the propitious moment. I've been off on Candy's arrival all week. What made me think I could get the time right with anyone else?

Hoss gets up abruptly from the sofa, tears streaming down his face as he disappears out the back door. Stay in the moment, damn you, even if it hurts. Ashok, rising effortlessly out of his cross-legged position, follows Hoss. Everything happens for a reason. You are where you need to be. It's all good. All the usual platitudes. Hoss is inconsolable, no doubt torn between wanting to sell the Wasteland to please his guru and moved to know what happened to his sister. Ask her forgiveness for the fog you've been in since she left, for doubting she would ever return.

Anthea and even Swann look uncomfortable, wishing they could have snuck out. Yet they seem perfectly in tune with their discomfort, sitting miserably together, a minor chord mother-and-child-reunion on the couch. A strange vantage point, standing here like this, in front of the screen. I can see what was once behind my back, or could if it were really there. Mary lighting her Tareyton. She never smoked upstairs. A quaint notion from the days of smoking sections in airplanes. It permeated, unfiltered, up the staircase and under the bedroom door, through the walls. I can still smell it, sometimes. Here, though, where it should be strongest, I sense nothing. No lethal scent, no ghostly presence. Now Swann and Anthea, too, have vanished. They were here only a moment ago.

40

RAIN POURS DOWN IN THE morning, wrecking the forecast of another sure thing.

Swann slips into the room while I'm ironing a suitable dress for Candy. Because even now she might surprise me. Sometimes I think: I haven't kept Candy alive; I've made her up. The images in *Going, going, gone*, and all the scenes played by Molly O, are more vivid than my memories. At the very least, I give them equal weight. Wouldn't that be a kick in the head, to find out I'm my own sister. Hitchcock should have filmed *Psycho* at the Wasteland. Norman Bates was his own mother. Has it come to this?

— I read your blog, man. It's really something. Especially after seeing your film. I just wasn't clear on why you think Candy is coming. Has she texted you?

— The steam smells funny. I shouldn't have used tap water. I wonder if the French use Perrier in their irons.

— Your brother is freaking out. He thinks you've lost

it. If you could give him some proof or something. That she's coming.

— Lost what?

— My mother is puffing all the time. I haven't seen her like this since her last breakup. She needs to feel helpful, and she doesn't know how. If you ask me, she's a Two, not a Four or a Six. I'm thinking I should see my dad. After the funeral.

Hoss cried because he thinks I'm nuts. This from a man with self-love affirmations stuck over his refrigerator and bathroom mirror in first, second, and third person. Say positive words often enough and they feel right. An inner sense of knowing takes over as one's psyche opens to a universal truth pushed away out of fear. Pitiful bullshit. How many sleepless nights has he endured, how many broken relationships, how many gurus and spiritual paths and healing journeys, how many retreats and workshops and sweat lodges. Despite his professed commitment to openness and non-judgment, he apparently can't fathom that Candy might have pursued a career as an actress, disappeared from sight, and become resurrected thanks to my blog. Or not. That's the thing.

I expected doubt and hostility from him, not tears of pity at his brother's questionable mental state. Swann's ambivalent response bothers me more. All I need do is give him something, anything, to hold on to his faith in me.

— Ashok likes the idea of a retreat centre right between Toronto and Montreal. My mother's dead against it. Going to that island was bad enough. Your place is just too far from Buffalo. She's trying to make him think about the Americans in his programs. Like no one ever thinks about us. I don't have the money for La Scala. I may end up singing in the shower.

The smouldering dress has set off the smoke alarm in the hall. Poisonous fumes seep out from under the iron. They surround us on Candy's bed, tease the tears out of our eyes.

41

OF COURSE THE BUZZES AND whistles return with a vengeance once Ashok takes up Flicker. He's got the magic touch. No aggression or impatience, he releases the plunger at exactly the right moment and doesn't sweat the things he can't control. His fingers stay poised on the flippers, relaxed but ready. His eyes do not stray up to the scoreboard because, after all, it's all about the process.

— I didn't see you standing there.

— I thought you'd have eyes in the back of your head. Don't stop on my account. You haven't won yet.

— It was a standing meditation. There's no winning. I feel you and I are like the balls in this machine. We have a moment of calm, and then we hit a rubber band, and all hell breaks loose.

— "Every moment for what it gives you." Isn't that what you preach?

— I'm sorry for what happened yesterday. It was my fault

227

for not speaking with you directly. And you're right. I knew nothing of your father's suffering. But I know something of your brother's.

Another meaningful glance in my direction. This man never indulges in half measures. His gaze is full bore, head-on with a veneer of friendliness and empathy that can't hide the intense, calculating mind underneath. His khaki pants and striped short-sleeved shirt would be innocuous on anyone else. On him they stand out as manipulations. And what's with the pinball? He was expecting me to drop in, and wanted to put up a front of normalcy. Yet I can easily see him fooling a mortgage advisor at the bank with his smooth, albeit heavily accented, patter. He'll wear a casual suit for the occasion and disguise his intentions. He wants a commercial, not a spiritual, property. They'll probably offer him cash-back. I can't afford to be wrong on this. I've been wrong too often this week.

— I enjoyed your presentation yesterday. It gave me a great deal of insight into your family, and what it meant to lose your sister.

— The key point was that I've found her.

— Your evidence was quite powerful.

I stop myself in the middle of a sharp comeback. Is this sincerity or another ploy to win my affections?

— So you'll understand why I don't want to sell the Wasteland to you.

— I did want to talk to you about all that.

— There's nothing to say. I'm not my brother. I don't want you anywhere near the scattering today. Am I clear?

He doesn't protest or acquiesce. Just stands there with an insufferable worldly look of unconditional acceptance.

— I asked Ashok to say a few words and play a few notes on his flute.

Hoss stands in the doorway of the barn, holding a velvet bag.

— I don't want him to talk, witness, observe, officiate, or take part in any way. I don't want his grimy hands anywhere near Joseph's remains.

— Cremains.

— You can't sell the Wasteland without my permission. I own half of it.

— I thought it was only a third.

The bag is heavier than expected, and when I strike his shoulder with it, Hoss almost tumbles over. He shoves me back, and I stagger up against Flicker. Joseph, meanwhile, or what's left of him, is rolling over and over before he reaches the grave. This can't end well. It will take a big man to make peace, bigger than either of us.

— Stop. I mean it.

Anthea's voice is uncompromisingly authoritative. Gone are the goofy gestures and run-on at the mouth. This must be the woman who raised Swann into a confident young man.

She opens the bag, and removes a small cardboard box with crushed corners. A plastic bag pokes out of a tear on one side. There's a label with Joseph's name and a coded number on the top. Even now, he's not a free man.

42

WE WALK SINGLE FILE TO the flat rock, equally spaced to give our umbrellas room to breathe and maintain the unspoken truce. Hoss leads, protecting the cremains beneath an ill-fitting, bring-me-back-alive windbreaker. Swann and Anthea follow, while I bring up the rear to make sure no one strays from the path. The downpour has awakened the mud and the rising steam has enveloped us in a thick fog. I keep checking over my shoulder. No Ashok in pursuit. Nor anyone else.

Standing in a circle under a roof of umbrellas, the four of us barely maintain eye contact. Soon enough their gazes all fall on me.

— I guess we can start.

Thunder shakes the sky with the force of a betrayal. If Joseph were here in more than spirit, he might chant to the Gods, bestow an ode upon his beloved wife or a plea to his missing daughter. Neither Hoss nor I could ever compete with that voice.

A sweet, otherworldly sound emanates from an unknown source. Slowly and quietly, at first, but then with increasing power and presence. Neither masculine nor feminine, a voice soars on top of the rain, drains the clouds of power, and leaves a caramel scent hanging in the air. Swann, singing "Forever Mozart" towards the heavens. La Scala is next indeed. Love this kid.

We fling open our fists onto the earth, over and over. I tell Joseph my last toss is for Candy, and let the gritty ash slip from my fingers. The heavens open anew, pounding the cremains and they disappear into the soil faster than quicksand. Hoss and Anthea tiptoe back to safety, away from the muck and rain, afraid to become infected with the virus they think has infiltrated my head. Swann waits, head cocked. I wave him off, and he leaves me alone on the rock.

It's a desolate place, really, even in the best of weather. In a downpour, the bleakness seems to rise out of the earth and soak into my pores. Is it really so important to save? All these years, I have held on to the past, scratching the wound at red lights and checkout lines and the back rows of cinemas. Discovering Molly O has propelled me to new extremes. Maybe I would have been better off in the dark. I know I'm right. Even Ashok said the evidence was compelling. But if Candy does not want to be found it all means nothing.

With Hoss's umbrella and one of Joseph's walking sticks, the guru makes his way out here. The slick mud, which has enveloped my shoes, will soil the ends of his khaki pants. When he falls, it will get into his beard, his hair, his eyes. His vision will blur from the rain and the fog. Disoriented, he will call my name, but I will throw my voice deeper into the field. Farther and farther he will travel, beyond the reach of any human hand, at the mercy of the shifting ground. The Wasteland will never accept the construction of a retreat centre.

Ashok is setting a remarkable pace for someone who's never set foot here before. I keep waiting for his knee to buckle or his body to sway. At the halfway point, I leave the flat rock and head deeper into the field. My footprints are immediately sucked up and disappear. Let's see how he fares off the beaten path.

I stumble twice, landing on my knees. Third time, I fall flat on my face. My right hand meets no resistance and I put it out quickly from the hole. Abandoning the umbrella, I crawl on all fours to measure the circumference of the quicksand. I wasn't aware of this one or else I'm disoriented. I wait a few feet back from the pit, covered in mud from head to toe. Al Jolson in blackface did not look more ridiculous. I raise my face to the skies for a cleansing.

Ashok continues with an insouciant air through the mud, as if out for a stroll in the merry, merry month of May. Never once looking back, never once slipping, never once doubting it makes perfect sense to be out here.

— Thank you for meeting me.

Those intolerably good manners! As if he accepts everything without judgment or curiosity. My filthy appearance is apparently neither here nor there.

— Inhospitable, your Wasteland.

— The place or its people?

He nods with amusement.

— When Janardan called the other day, his voice was distraught. He was not himself. He said your father had died, and he asked me to come here. He was adamant. I sensed something would unfold so I agreed. I don't regret my decision, although it's been difficult for both of you.

— Hoss was himself long before he met you.

He nods again, this time more ruefully.

— He will get tired of Momentous Moments, and look for something new.

— Possibly. But that does not detract from its value today.

— He can't sell without my permission.

— And your sister's. Don't forget her.

I stare at his face for any trace of derision. Nothing.

— If you still want to say a few words, then maybe share that thought with my brother. He doesn't believe Candy is Molly O.

— Is that what he doesn't believe?

— He thinks she's no longer alive, is that it? Which would explain why we haven't heard from her. I don't buy that. You don't either. Or you wouldn't keep bringing her up. Correct?

Ashok bends down, dangerously close to the quicksand pit, and picks up a clump of sloppy mud. He lets it slip through his fingers. Then he shrugs. Not out of callous indifference to Candy's fate. It's more a gesture of helplessness in the face of what we can't and don't know. I want to dive at his feet to save those drops of mud from disappearing into the muck of the earth.

— My mother and now my father are part of this land.

Their ashes were scattered here. This entire field is a memorial to them. I won't give it up without a fight.

— Janardan has told me the stories about the quicksand.

— You don't think it's real.

— Do you?

— I have to believe in it.

A bolt of thunder covers the crack in my voice.

— Why is that?

— Because if the quicksand exists so does Candy.

The words sound like a foreign tongue. Did I think them or say them aloud?

— And if there's no quicksand?

— There is.

— I came out here to tell you I'm no longer interested in the Wasteland. In many ways, it's the perfect setting. But it doesn't feel right. Apart from the conflict it's creating between you and Janardan, there is a presence here, a palpable resistance in the soil. Other souls linger. Not just your parents. You feel them, too. They might be reassured in time, but perhaps not. My intuition tells me to leave them be.

My mouth hangs open stupidly.

— Why didn't you say that ten minutes ago?

— You needed to tell me about the quicksand. Can we shake hands?

His abrupt movement snaps me out of my dream state. I remember the danger. I can't have murder on my conscience, not when he's proven himself to be a pretty decent fellow. But he's too quick. He steps forward, hand outstretched. I wait for the dreaded sucking sound, for panic to replace the eternal calm on his face. His desperate leap to the edge will fail, leaving him waist-deep in the shifting sands. The walking stick will smack pointlessly against the mud. He will hold it out to me in desperation, but it will fall short. This is the most momentous moment of all. He realizes a lifetime of moving with the energy flow, of accepting all that is, has been wasted. A lie he told himself, and charged others good money to hear. For in the struggle against death he has never felt so alive. If only he could survive to share this insight! He would structure his entire teachings around it.

His bare feet are not sucked up and dragged down. His palm is not damp with expectancy. It feels normal.

43

HOSS STARTS UP A CHANT to sell the broken Predicta. Dried mud from Little Joe Grant's dive in the field thrown in for nothing. It's funny for a few seconds. Then both of us feel Joseph's absence. I still prefer laughter to silence, and the reminder of Mary and Candy and all they didn't say.

Hoss gets up from the stage, and paces around.

— It used to be the new shows all started in the fall. It was something to look forward to. Now they're coming out all the time, all summer long. So many channels. I can't keep up.

The ache in his voice almost brings me to tears.

— What's with all those tapes of *All My Children*?

— Beats me.

— I'm sorry about the blackboard.

— Me too.

My response sounds more like a lament for Hoss's idiocy than an apology for my role in the debacle. Our moment of brotherly bonding is ebbing. We walk together in silence towards the front of the house, and then he continues to his car alone. Ashok dons shades to combat the burst of afternoon sunshine, while Anthea adds one last layer of protection to her face. It only takes a few seconds for them to disappear. In the distance, Hoss honks out the opening notes of "Aqualung" as a late peace-making gesture. Something to build on.

Swann and I repair to the wicker chairs on the verandah. If we're really to spend August here together, I need to buy a hammock. Swann needs time to think about college or save money for a trip to Italy.

— I was thinking we could mount an opera about Molly O. You could write the words. I would write the music and sing. You could film it and make a mashup with the Mickey Nailand clips. A multimedia extravaganza. We could make it a fundraiser to get me to La Scala.

— Maybe we could dust off the old Steenbeck in the barn.

— Digital, man. We need to go digital.

It's a joke, I want to tell him, a reference to those wholesome Andy Hardy movies. He's probably never heard of Mickey Rooney, let alone seen him put on a show.

Swann could help with the lyrics. We'd have Candy's wardrobe to draw upon. I could slap a fresh coat of varnish on the stage and mend holes in the canvas roof. Auctiongoers were used to standing for hours, but we could rent chairs for our performance. We'd promote it with posters on hydro poles in the village. Maybe build a secure website for donations. Upload a demo on Facebook and YouTube. It could go viral.

44

THUNDER RUMBLES EVER CLOSER, THREATENING a downpour to break the humidity. The flat rock is only a few inches above the ground, hardly high enough to prevent streams of fast-flowing mud from attacking the tent. In the distance, a light from Candy's room, but I know it's just Swann.

I don't expect to find her tonight. I'm here out of habit more than conviction.

The flashlight has dropped out of my hands and rolled off, the batteries dead or extinguished from contact with the earth. I smell the rain before I feel or hear it. Sweet and humid. A sharp flash in the sky and it pours down. There is nowhere to run. If only I could shoot up a flare.

On the east side of the path, a quicksand pit. I can't bring myself to test it with my stick. I'm afraid nothing will happen.

I STARE INTO the far reaches of the Wasteland, beyond where any of us have dared tread, in case a flash of lightning reveals a small figure moving steadily across the field. The going would be treacherous in the slippery mud, the path far from certain. I'm almost relieved to see no one. The rain ramps up its intensity, and I strip off my wet clothes, intending to spread them on the boulders behind the tent for the early morning sun. There are already clothes here, carefully laid out. Women's clothes.

She can barely hold her own against the bracing wind that maliciously impedes her progress. Two bolts of lightning crack open the earth on either side of her narrow path, creating jagged abysses. The driving rain stings her face, blinds her vision, loosens her footing. The Wasteland is punishing her for the long absence, forcing her to earn the right of return.

AS I APPROACH the sleeping bag, a wave of caramel, vanilla, and musky flannel envelops me.

— I said I'd come back.

The voice, strangely familiar. Deeper than I had imagined. She turns to face me in the dark. Her breasts brush up against my chest. They are recognizably large.

— Rox.

— You were expecting someone else?

— You're wearing Candy.

This is all she's wearing, the first time I've seen her near a bed without four layers. Her long mess of hair has been cut and shaped, falling casually across her forehead. This is both Rox and not Rox.

We talk on our sides, elbows pressed against the thin

mattress. Lightning illuminates our faces for a second every few minutes, not enough to make us uncomfortable. That will come when the sun streams onto our naked bodies and we have to fetch our clothes outside.

— You came out here once before. For a sleepover. I watched from the house.

— She liked the silence. The isolation. The desolation.

— We never talk about her.

— Why is that, do you think?

Rox turns her back towards me again, retreats to the farthest reaches of the sleeping bag. The imprint of her warm body has disappeared from the length of flannel next to me, and the space has already gone cold. The vibrations of her laugh are nothing compared to her unfiltered tears. If I'm not careful, the pounding will crack my heart right open.

— The way you looked at me after my shower. I thought we were both ready to let her go.

In an episode of *Gunsmoke*, a rattlesnake crawls into Marshall Dillon's sleeping bag while he's camping in the wild. They have to pull the bag off him and shoot the snake before it can bite, all in one swift motion. That's nothing compared to the savage and single-minded manner in which Rox flings off the sleeping bag and leaves me defenceless. She steps over my legs, crouching towards the flap. The zipper is jammed tight. She tugs, pulls, and curses.

— Your flashlight's right here.

— Don't you dare turn it on.

Go then, Lady Godiva. If you're not ready for your

close-up, strut naked up the third concession in the pelting rain. There are no shelters from this storm. Not since you ripped down Candy's words from the wall.

She retreats to a corner and collapses. Was that a crack of thunder or the snap of my heart string?

— You're leaving again.

— You're not stopping me again.

— That polyethylene floor must be damp and unpleasant.

— It's stuck to my ass if you want to know.

— Come back.

My sexual relations have followed the conventions of classical linear narrative — from title sequence to end-credits, in that order and usually within the allotted ninety minutes. Every gesture and gasp, every stroke and sigh, has already been written, rehearsed, and played out many times before. My lovemaking with Rox is unscripted. I keep my eyes closed as she leaves before the lights come up.

45

ON THE TOP TIER OF the stage, under a corner of the canvas that still holds off rain, I put my back to the Wasteland and take an auctioneer's view of the landscape. Stormy weather turns away the casual crowds, leaving hardcore patrons who stand defiantly in their slickers, refusing to be suckered into paying too much because of a little water. Joseph has to compete against their iron will and the sound of the pounding rain, all without a microphone. With a slight change in intonation, his honey-bathed voice places these grown men into strollers where they stare up into the loving eyes of their mothers. Squatting beneath him in our hideout, protected from the rain by the tarp overhead, Candy and I hold our mouths open under the cracks of the boards to let the chant soothe our fears.

ACKNOWLEDGEMENTS

I thank the Canada Council for the Arts, which provided funds for the writing of this book.

Through the Quebec Writers' Federation, I met Marc Côté, editor and publisher of Cormorant Books, whose guidance was vital for *Molly O* to achieve its final shape.

I am grateful to MM Serra, executive director of the Film-makers' Cooperative in New York, who gave me much insight into the workings of the cooperative and the experimental film scene in New York during the 1980s and 1990s. In addition, she steered me towards *captured: a film/video history of the lower east side* by Clayton Patterson (Seven Stories Press, New York, 2005), which helped me situate the apocryphal films of Mickey Nailand and Molly O.

Lee Goldberg's *Unsold Television Pilots 1955 through 1989* (McFarland & Company, Jefferson, North Carolina, 1990) offered a window into what might have been that fed my imagination.

MOLLY O

Most of all I am indebted to Michka Saäl for her astute suggestions, her unflagging belief in this book, and everything else.